SIGNET VISTA • 451-AE2254 • $2.50

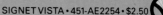

Being a preacher's kid is kind of special—but sometimes
special is a hard thing to be . . . "Compelling characters . . .
provocative reading."—<u>School Library Journal</u>

What I Really
Think Of You

M. E. KERR

Best Selling Author Of
DINKY HOCKER SHOOTS SMACK! &
IF I LOVE YOU, AM I TRAPPED FOREVER?

TALKING TONGUES . . .

Once, in the cafeteria at Central High, six or seven of you plunked yourselves down at my table.

"Opal," one of you started in, "I hear down at your church you do something called talking in tongues. Can you talk in tongues, Opal?"

"Let's hear it, Opal."

"Is it like this, Opal? Cook a look a book a dook a duck."

All getting into the act, laughing, speaking gibberish . . .

Daddy told me that night, "They was just curious, Opal."

My brother Bobby John said, "Just keep your mouth shut, Opal. That's all you can do."

"They don't know anything down to that high school," Mum said. "Just tell them once your own mum thought the whole idea of tongues was funny as a chicken with its head off until the day she seen the light."

"Them high school kids aren't interested in tongues," Bobby John said. "They're out to get you!"

"Then get them back!" Daddy shouted.

That was easy for her dad to say, but Opal didn't know the first thing about getting back at anybody . . .

WHAT I REALLY THINK OF YOU

More Great Fiction from SIGNET VISTA

WHAT I REALLY THINK OF YOU

by
M. E. Kerr

A SIGNET VISTA BOOK
NEW AMERICAN LIBRARY
TIMES MIRROR

PUBLISHER'S NOTE

This novel is a work of fiction. Names, characters, places, and
incidents are either the product of the author's imagination or are
used fictitiously, and any resemblance to actual persons, living or
dead, events, or locales is entirely coincidental.

RL 5/IL 7+

Copyright © 1982 by M. E. Kerr

This is an authorized reprint of a hardcover edition published by
Harper & Row, Publishers, Inc. A hardcover edition was published
simultaneously in Canada by Fitzhenry & Whiteside Limited,
Toronto.

SIGNET VISTA TRADEMARK REG. U.S. PAT. OFF. AND FOREIGN COUNTRIES
REGISTERED TRADEMARK—MARCA REGISTRADA
HECHO EN CHICAGO, U.S.A.

SIGNET, SIGNET CLASSICS, MENTOR, PLUME, MERIDIAN AND NAL
BOOKS are published by The New American Library, Inc.,
1633 Broadway, New York, New York 10019

First Signet Vista Printing, April, 1983

3 4 5 6 7 8 9

PRINTED IN THE UNITED STATES OF AMERICA

To my friend and agent,
Patricia Schartle Myrer—
with deep appreciation

One

OPAL RINGER

If I was to say that finally Opal Ringer is going to tell you what she really thinks of you, would you laugh?

You always used to laugh. I never had to do much more than just show up and you'd all start nudging each other with grins starting to tip your mouths.

Now you come to see me, and I pretend I don't particularly see you, but I see every one of your faces.

I know all your faces so well.

I see every face out there but one.

He doesn't come. I think he wants to, but I know he won't.

I start my story with the day I first saw Jesse Pegler. That was when my whole life first started changing.

You were all in my life for longer than I like to remember. You never changed me, just made me dig deeper under my strangeness, made me pull the crazy blanket over my head to look out at your real world through eye slits.

But Jesse Pegler brought me just a little closer to your world.

If any of you say to yourselves, "Did you ever think Opal Ringer would be famous for anything?"

remember that I wouldn't have, the way you always thought I wouldn't have, if it hadn't been for a certain Sunday at the end of May.

Woke up to hear my brother, Bobby John, arguing with Daddy over who'd get which bumper sticker.

Daddy already had three of them things plastered on the back of our van, one saying I KNOW THE WAY IF YOU ARE LOST, one saying HONK IF YOU LOVE JESUS, one saying COME TO THE HAND FOR A HAND.

The Hand is Daddy's church: The Helping Hand Tabernacle.

Daddy and Bobby John like bumper stickers the way Mum likes Good & Plenty candy and I like nice things. More about me and nice things later, but now is not the time.

I went downstairs in my robe and got a glass of milk out of the refrigerator.

They were all at the table in the kitchen, where these two new bumper stickers were sitting, still in their cellophane wrappers.

Mum said to Bobby John to take the green-and-white one because his car was green.

"The green-and-white one happens to be the one I want," said my daddy. (The green-and-white one said FAMOUS LAST WORDS: DON'T BUG ME ABOUT JESUS.)

Mum said, "I don't even know what it means."

"What'd you buy it for if you don't know what it means, Arnelle?"

"What it means," said Bobby John, "is that some fellow is resisting Jesus. Some fellow is saying, 'Hey, don't bug me about Jesus!' And he's an inch from being saved."

"Oh, I know that," Mum said.

"You just got through saying you didn't," said Daddy.

"Royal," Mum said to him, "take the blue-and-white one. Why won't you just take the blue-and-white one?"

(The blue-and-white one said YOU REALLY DO ONLY GO AROUND IN LIFE ONCE, SO GO WITH JESUS.)

Daddy started talking about how Bobby John was spoiled clear rotten and thought he could get his way in anything. Daddy said a child should be beholden to his father, never mind that Bobby John was nineteen years old.

I gave the cat some of my milk in a saucer on the linoleum floor, and parked myself on the kitchen stool.

Then I started doing it again: Watching everything including me as though I had a spirit in me could leave my body and look down at myself.

Down at The Hand they'd make something out of it if I was to tell them, say I was having an out-of-body experience or some dumb thing.

I looked at the room.

I saw me on the stool first. I was sixteen, and had black hair falling past my shoulders and light-brown eyes. Had the pale face all Ringers have. Look like ghosts. I was famous for not smiling, and more famous for not talking a lot when there was more than one person around. Seems like there always was, so you wouldn't have called me a mouth.

Daddy was the mouth. Well, he had to be, being a preacher. He was a big man but skinny, and his thick black eyebrows met at a point on his nose. He looked fierce, put the fear of God in you. Well, he was supposed to. But Mum said remember to smile. Royal, now you got a nice smile, and the little ones come to services have to see that smile or they're going to cry. You point too much, Mum said, you point when you shout, and those little tykes don't know they didn't do nothing wrong. You scare them, Royal.

I've never seen Daddy in anything but a white shirt and dark pants, tie sometimes, sometimes not, but he wouldn't put a colored shirt on his back if the Devil was about to eat him.

One thing he liked was nice coat linings. He liked the satiny kind, red, silver, black, gold. When he

opened his coat and waved his arms around, you'd
see the lining and it was real nice.

Bobby John looked like Daddy, was what you'd call
the spitting image. But he was not Daddy and never
would be, and that was what made his life hard, I
guess. He was supposed to be following in Daddy's
foosteps, but it was like an ant trying to put his legs
down in elephant tracks.

Bobby John had the same coal-colored, bushy hair,
and the same bright-blue eyes, and he was as tall,
but give him a sermon to preach and folks found
places to scratch, worked their jaws hard to keep
from yawning, and took peeks at their wristwatches.
Bobby John knew it, and got worse as he went along.
His nerve ran out on him, like a cat running from the
fleas on her own back, and all you wanted to say was
somebody get that poor boy down from up there. You
thought of Bobby John as a boy. We all did.

When we were little, it was always Bobby John
who told me stories about the Devil. Anything to do
with the Devil got to Bobby John. His very favorite
Bible story was about the pigs who committed suicide: At the Sea of Galilee, Jesus met two men whose
bodies were filled by devils. The devils were afraid
Jesus would get them out, so they asked Jesus to let
them go into the bodies of pigs in a nearby herd.
Jesus let them do it, but it drove the pigs crazy and
they drowned themselves in a lake.

Anytime Bobby John got himself into trouble, he
said he knew he was going to, because right before
he did he felt something heavy inside him. Said it had
to be Satan himself.

Daddy'd tell Bobby John Satan had bigger things
up his sleeve than all the dumb little things Bobby
John did, but Bobby John stuck to his story.

One thing Bobby John was, was stubborn, and I
gave him credit that morning for fighting Daddy.
There was no way he was going to get that bumper
sticker he wanted, if Daddy didn't want him to have
it, but he sat their insisting, while Daddy'd say half

the time Bobby John couldn't even get his car to run. Work on getting that car to run, Daddy'd say, never mind what you want the back end to say. If that bumper sticker was on your car, Daddy'd say, half the time no one'd see the thing but the cat out in the backyard.

I loved Bobby John for trying, cringed every time Daddy shamed him by bad-mouthing him and calling him "boy."

Then Mum.

Arnelle Watson Ringer, born and raised in the Tennessee mountains, pretty as a picture in her day, but fat and back to not liking to wear shoes if she didn't have to.

She was a secret listener to records of Dolly Parton, Loretta Lynn, and Crystal Gale, and would any day rather hear Loretta sing "It Wasn't God Who Made Honky Tonk Angels" than a whole heavenly choir sing "Abide with Me."

She could sing a mean song herself, but since she got so fat wouldn't solo no more, stayed up with the choir. Anyway, I'd have rather caught her voice coming from the bathroom, when she was soaking in the tub, crying out "I Knew You When" like she still weighed 116 pounds and had love problems.

My own voice was real good, too, but the shaking in my knees wouldn't quit and I'd like to faint before I got up in front of anybody.

Mum was the one I told some of my troubles to, when and if I told them at all. She'd put her arms around me after a while and say, "Well now shush. Hush, honey," as though hearing me pained her as much as what I was telling her hurt me. Her green eyes teared and she laughed as though her eyes weren't ever supposed to leak unless she was seeing hungry mouths or twisted bodies. Patted me. Said, "Hush. Shush," waited for me to be finished.

One time when I was real little Mum and I had a talk about bumper stickers and the van. On the sides of the van JESUS IS COMING was written in letters so big you'd thought they were advertising the message to giants. Plus the van was rusting and painted pink, and had a speaker to play recorded hymns over.

Mum said, "What're you, ashamed to go in it?"

"Well, I just feel like everybody's looking."

"We want them to look, honey."

"I know you do. You blast that music so's no one'd have a choice anyhow."

"Do you get teased about it at school? Is that it?"

"I know they talk behind my back."

"What do you think they say? They say we love Jesus."

"That ain't what they say."

"Don't say 'ain't,' honey. I know you get that from me and I apologize. What do you think they say, Opal?"

"Say we're Holy Rollers."

"They don't say we're robbers. They don't say we're adulterers. They don't say we're liars. Now, if they was saying we was robbers, and adulterers and liars, then I'd like to hide my face along with you, but Opal Ringer, what they're saying is we're slain in the spirit!"

"They don't even know what slain in the spirit means!"

"Well, they know we love Jesus."

"They know we got Jesus' name all over our van is what they know, and that's not painted all over their cars."

"You're a preacher's child, Opal Ringer. It has its pain but it has its joy, too. Tell me you'll never find your daddy coming up the front walk with a load on, and right there you're ahead of the crowd."

"Okay," I said. "Forget it."

"Oh hush. Shush. I know. I know." Hugging me hard. "We ain't living our lives for what a bunch of snotty school kids think of us, honey."

"You're telling me we're not," I said.

But right before I met Jesse, I'd about made my

peace with being a preacher's child. I'd almost come to not care.

That Sunday morning while I drank my milk on the kitchen stool, and watched my father win the argument over who got the bumper sticker, I was planning what I'd wear to The Hand.

I was accepting that it'd be just another Sunday.

I wasn't looking for anything special out of that May day.

That's when things happen, you know. Things happen when you're not expecting them.

And something else I'm bound to say: While these certains things are just beginning to happen, your dumb mind doesn't even know it right away.

Your dumb mind doesn't even give you any warning that your whole life is about to change.

That's what amazes me.

Two

JESSE PEGLER

My name is Jesse Pegler. The most important thing about me has always been who my father is. There were things I couldn't do because of who my father is, and things I had to do for the same reason.

Before he got on TV, you had to drive to the outskirts of your town to see him, unless you were in the jail or the hospital. Then he'd sometimes come right to your cell or your bed on the ward. But most people had to get on a bus or in a car and go out to where our advance men had pitched our tent with the letters the size of fence posts on both sides proclaiming:

BROTHER PEGLER, EVANGELIST FOR JESUS!

People would be streaming in from all points those Sunday nights, and my brother, Bud, would be warming them up with "The Old Rugged Cross," "God Sent His Son," or "Put Your Hand in the Hand of the Man from Galilee." The Challenge Choir would be backing Bud up, though Bud never needed them for support. Bud never needed help shining: He was a born star.

My mother and I would be in our Sunday best, sitting in the front row, and my father would be out behind the tent pacing and praying in his shirt sleeves until he got the cue from the choir, telling him the tent was filled to overflowing and it was time to put on his jacket and get out there.

The cue was the first chorus of "Farther Along." I always got excited when I heard it, knowing he'd be out any second. I always got goose bumps, knowing he'd be dynamite, blast them sky-high with his preaching.

He did, too. He does.

My father always liked to say he was just a tent preacher. He still said it sometimes, although his tack was changed like his tent.

You might have seen my father on television. He's there in living color every Sunday morning, sandwiched between cartoons and politicians being interviewed by the press.

If you have seen him on TV, you probably haven't forgotten him. How do you forget a minister in blue robes with gold tassels running up a white staircase to a white-and-gold balcony overlooking the Atlantic Ocean? When he reaches the top, while he catches his breath and holds his hands palms up, eyes squeezed shut, the TV screen explodes in a riot of color and organ chords, as though the picture tube was about to blow, and you see:

GUY PEGLER

IT'S UP TO

  YOU! GUY PEGLER GUY PEGLER IT'S UP

  TO

  YOU you you you you you

  guy guy guy guy guy guy

PEGLER!

Then my old man turns around, blond hair blowing in the wind, blue eyes sparkling behind big black owl glasses, white teeth flashing his big, broad smile, and his voice booms: "JE-SUS wants YOU to win! So do I!"

The Challenge Choir comes in at that point chorusing:

"Run, climb, reach for a star!
You make your-self what you are.
Where there's a will, there's a way—
Win one with Jesus today!"

On this particular morning at the end of May, my father began his sermon (he calls them "challenges") with a quote from a poet called Edgar Guest:

"Somebody said that it couldn't be done,
But he with a chuckle replied
That maybe it couldn't, but he would be one
Who wouldn't say no till he's tried."

Seal von Hennig and I were watching the service on the TV in my father's study.

"Do you want a Coke?" I asked her.

"I want my teeth more. You're never going to have your dad's smile if you keep on drinking Coke around the clock."

"Just what I always wanted," I said, "his smile. I could live without looking like either one of them."

I was always being compared to my dad or Bud.

Bud was the whole reason Seal was there that morning. It was the closest she could come to being near him.

My sixteenth birthday was a real event. It was the day Bud ran away. It was also the last time my father ever preached a sermon under the tent, and it was the first time he didn't preach as Brother Pegler. He became Dr. Guy Pegler; the Dr. was an honorary degree from a Bible college.

For a horrible three minutes he dragged me in front of the cameras. He told all the Boob Tube Land I was his youngest son, and then he asked everyone if I wasn't really a chip off the old block, look how good-looking I was. We stood there, the two of us, sandy-haired and blue-eyed and tanned from the hot summer sun.

The entire live audience applauded. There were probably plenty of viewers at home ready to barf, but we only heard from them by mail, long after the moment had passed, and we didn't see all the mail that poured in, anyway.

"Yes, Lord, thank you for this boy! I love him! I love him!" my father shouted out with his arms raised up. "I love him!"

No mention of Number One Son, naturally.

That was who my father really loved. And my mother. And Seal.

I guess the thing Seal von Hennig was most known for in Seaville was attending the Seaville High Spring Hop with a snake wrapped around her neck. It was the only time I didn't wish she was my date instead of Bud's. My mother said if there was a stray dog or a lost cat within a five-mile radius of Seaville, Seal'd find it somehow and cart it home.

Seal was at the tail end of a thing with Eddie Eden, whose father was a conservationist and ran an animal preserve. He'd lent her this snake named Passion, and all through the Hop it was hanging down her back, the forked tongue flicking away. Bud just grinned. Nothing ever bothered Bud, not even the fact Eddie had lent her Passion.

It was because of Eddie that Seal became the St. Francis of Seaville High, committed to the care and salvation of all animal life. Her real name was Sally von Hennig, but she got the nickname her freshman year when she was busy taking around petitions to protest the seal hunt off the coast of Labrador. She was after the kids to stop their mothers from buying fur coats, and she organized a picket line in front of Cross Hardware when they stocked traps for raccoons and squirrels.

My father said what Seal did was really commendable, not just because it was humane but because it was unusual for someone as rich and beautiful as Seal

to be so altruistic. I wasn't sure how unusual that
was, but I did know Seal always got gung ho on any
subject that interested the boy she was dating. She
was known for that around Seaville.

My father used to tell Bud he chose well, and after
Bud left, my father said he hoped Bud realized what
he gave up when he told Seal good-bye.

Seal acted like she hadn't heard Bud right. She was
always at our house, and still so taken up with ACE my
father was ready to put her on staff. ACE stood for
A Challenge Enterprise, our official name.

It was our second summer on TV, our first in The
Summer House.

Even though we were almost at the tip of Long
Island, on Sunday mornings traffic would pour into
Seaville from as far away as New York City, New
Jersey, and Connecticut.

The cars in our parking lot were bumper to bumper
all the way back by noon, when my father's picture
came on the enormous screen across from the balcony
where he stood, and his voice thundered across the
loudspeakers.

The few hundred people who didn't watch him in
their cars had to be in their seats in The Summer
House by ten-thirty, long before the TV crew arrived. Everyone drew lots before they climbed the
steps up to The Summer House, to see who would be
among the lucky dozen to be televised shaking his
hand after.

Winters, my father wrote and lectured and trav-
eled around the country with The Challenge Choir,
staging Winning Rallies.

Even though I looked like my father (and enough
like Bud to be his shorter twin), I was a somnanbulant
version of him—that's what my father called me. According to him, the "him" in me had not been awak-
ened yet. He claimed I still made wishes instead of
plans, and said if I didn't decide what I wanted to be,
it might be too late when I got around to it.

Bud was the chip off the old block before he split.

He was the follower in my father's footsteps, go-getter, ball of fire. Bud and Seal had all sorts of plans for when Bud would become a preacher. Seal had his same kind of energy and enthusiasm, and like Bud she was tall and blond, and people turned around for a second look. She had green eyes that sparkled and a way of moving that was quick and graceful, and she always seemed to be excited about something—Bud used to tell her she was filled with schemes and dreams, and chuck her under the chin with his thumb until she'd protest, "*Listen* to me! I'm serious!"

"Well, then, you be the preacher," he'd say. "You're the one with the business head, and your daddy could buy you a church!"

Right before Bud cut out he said things like that to Seal a lot. He'd go after our father, too, accusing him of turning religion into big business.

"It *is* big business," my father'd answer.

Bud would mutter, "Then count me out."

"Should the Lord's work be some two-bit opera-tion?" My father.

Bud would shout back that there was a limit, then he'd storm out of the house and my father'd say he was probably going to cool off over in the von Hennigs' big swimming pool.

Bud claimed my father would sit down and listen to any idea a von Hennig had, but I think what he was really steamed about was that Seal's ideas were good ones. Bud couldn't stand not being the star. Since I could remember, he always wanted to be in the cen-ter of the room. That was hard around Seal.

That Sunday morning Seal was excited about a way to improve our "Personality Segment."

We called it the P.S.

It was a five-minute segment which featured some-one who'd overcome adversity. Most of the time my father's staff found someone from the mailbag, who'd written in for one of the charms he gave away period-ically. It could be a gold ladder, or a gold C for Challenge, a gold star ("Shine and twinkle!") or, as it was that Sunday, a gold nutshell with a crack in it ("If you don't crack the shell, you can't eat the nut" was his morning message).

Often the people who wrote in for the charms had inspiring stories. My father would send an ACE scout to interview them. If the scout found a likely candidate, my father would ship whoever it was into Seaville for the P.S.

"Jesse, I just thought of an idea!" Seal said. "Do you know Opal Ringer? Her father runs The Helping Hand Tabernacle?" She didn't wait for my answer but got to her feet, pulling her long hair back from her face. "Opal and her mother work for us, and last night Arnelle said they're having a healing this afternoon!"

I was watching the end of the P.S. on TV. A heroin addict from Atlanta, Georgia, had just told how he kicked his habit when he became a Born-Again Christian. The choir was starting to sing "What a Difference You've Made in My Life."

I could hear the car motors turn over out in the lot. A lot of our auto viewers didn't wait for the Glory Be, to get started ahead of the traffic.

"Jesse, what about getting someone from right here in Seaville for the P.S.? What about getting someone who's been healed?"

"Have you ever been to one of those things, Seal?"

"It's a really neat idea! Your father's always saying he wants to do more for the local churches!"

She didn't answer my question; she didn't have to. Seal always went to church where the floors were carpeted and the kneeling benches padded.

"It's a super idea!" she congratulated herself.

I felt like telling her to knock it off—Bud was finished with her, and nothing she could do for ACE would change that. He'd told me himself the thing with Seal had ended for him; he pinpointed the ending to an evening when she'd stopped him in the middle of this long, passionate kiss to tell him about some new idea she had for "telephone tithing."

I began to get that ache in my gut that came when I watched Seal and realized she never saw me. She looked at me but I wasn't there: Bud's brother was.

She was hopping around the room now in her stocking feet and jeans and T-shirt, telling me of course I know who Opal Ringer was when I didn't, going on and on the way Seal did.

I was wondering why we couldn't just roll up our jeans around our ankles and run down to the beach, along the surf, hand in hand, and talk about something simple like who did what at school, laughing and forgetting everything back at ACE.

I was always wondering things like that, missing being something like a plumber's son or the son of a lawyer, or anything but a preacher's kid. We could never just roll around on the floor with the comics Sunday mornings and let the world go by.

"Seal?" I said. "Why don't we just roll up our jeans and—"

"Shhh! Jesse."

My father's face appeared bigger than life on the TV, and his voice echoed from the loudspeakers outside. "Glory be to the Father, and to the Son, and—"

I sighed and held my chin with my hands, while Seal stood as still as she could and still be Seal, shut her eyes, bowed her head.

"Amen!" my father said.

"Jesse?" Seal said, coming across to me and throwing herself across my lap. "You want to go for a ride?"

"Hey! What're you doing?"

She mussed up my hair with her long fingers.

"What're you *doing*, Seal?"

"Getting you to go to a healing with me," Seal said. "I'll even let you drive."

Three

OPAL RINGER

I used to hate it when anyone from your world showed up at The Hand. It wasn't anything I ever had to worry about a lot, because those of you who did go to church went to the fancy ones along Main Street, or out to the new TV Summer House, starring Guy Pegler.

Seaville had eight churches beside ours and one Jewish Center. All of them were on the other side of the railroad tracks from us. Even the black Baptist church was located on the good side of the tracks.

We were down in The Hollow, a stone's throw from the dump.

On a hot Sunday morning when we had the doors and windows open, you could hear the gulls fighting over the garbage. When the wind blew you could smell the garbage, too.

I'll never forget the time Mr. Westminster brought the whole Central High social history class to The Hand. Seeing how the Holy Rollers roll, I guess, calling it studying the ways others worship or some dumb thing like that. Daddy was glad because the offering was over three hundred dollars that Sunday. . . . Me, I wished I was six foot under. I felt like I was walking around in front of all of you in my underwear.

I remember the looks on your faces. Every time

16

somebody'd raise their palms and say, "Thank you, Jesus!" you'd give each other looks, and your mouths would start twitching. You'd pretend you were coughing behind your hands, and a couple of you couldn't even fake it, just got to giggling.

Every Sunday someone got slain in the spirit and fell over. Some churches had catchers, men who stood by to help the fall of whoever it was keeled over. Daddy didn't believe in that, believed no one got hurt when the spirit of Jesus moved him or her. No one ever came up from the floor in The Hand worse off than before they fell, so maybe Daddy was onto something.

But you all never saw anything like that in your lives. I remember it scared Sybil Younger so bad she ran down the aisle and out the back door.

The woman who fell was Mrs. Bunch from Bunch Cleaners. She got slain in the spirit three or four times a year, and she was big, landed with a thud. Daddy always went over and stood by her and said, "Oh thank you, Jesus!" and the rest of us said it, too.

Sometimes I said it and sometimes I didn't, and I sure didn't say it that Sunday morning. My face was the color of cooked beets, and I didn't even have Mum to hide behind. She was up there with her slip showing in the front row of the choir, singing "When God Dips His Love in My Heart."

That Sunday afternoon before the healing, there was one of you waiting out front when we came up from lunch in the basement. On healing Sundays we always brought lunch so people didn't have to troop home and back on the same day.

My own personal name for Seal von Hennig was V. Chicken. She was one of them who went to Seaville High, the school kids going on to college attend.

Before Bud Pegler ran off from home, Seal was his girl and they were the IT couple in this whole town. They had IT and they were IT, and you know how you watch a pair like them and think about what they got, what it'd be like to be them.

I knew more about what was between them than most, I think, because I helped out at the von Hennigs' when Mum couldn't handle all the work herself. Mum earned extra money working there, said I didn't do any helping out holding their lace tablecloths to my face, swooning over the way they felt against my skin, but some of the stuff the von Hennigs had over to their place I'd never seen the likes of.

Daddy said sometimes he thought it was Satan's doing that I loved nice things the way I did, because who'd I ever get that from? I had no real answer to that one. Seemed like I was born with that love like I was born with black hair and brown eyes: Seemed like a part of me missing, the way a body'd miss one of its arms.

Truth is I probably got it from the von Hennigs themselves, being up there like I was when I was little, tagging after Mum from room to room in that place. You could have set our whole house down in their dining room/kitchern/pantry and have room for a ping-pong table besides.

It was up to their place I got my first glimpse of Bud Pegler and her, up to their place I got to know him some. I wrote down word for word one thing Bud Pegler said to me, leaning down to say it with the grin on his face and his eyes staring into mine, his mouth so close to mine I felt his warm breath on my lips.

"Opal, you've got real pretty eyes, and someday—"

I never liked V. Chicken, even though she never personally did anything to me. She even sent down some of her clothes for me to wear. I never wanted to go up and thank her for them, so Mum made me writer her thank-you notes instead. I'd complain and complain, and Daddy said to call her up on the telephone if writing notes was so hard. I'd say, "I wouldn't call her up if you paid me."

"Well, no good deed goes unpunished," Daddy'd

say. "Girl sends some pretty things down to you and winds up on your hate list."

"I don't have no hate list."

"Don't sound like you like her, Opal, and I hope the reason's not envy."

Deep down I couldn't cross off envy as the reason, but I wasn't telling him that. Told him I didn't have a reason, sometimes you just don't take to someone, but I knew as well as I knew how to spell Satan I sometimes hated being a have-not. I'd have been a real good have, and not taken none of it for granted the way V. Chicken did. I don't think she thought twice about being a have, and I know personlly from looking in her closets there was clothes on hangers with the price tags still on them, just never got around to wearing them.

V. Chicken was her beautiful self that May morning standing out in front of The Hand. Times I was up there working, I didn't run into her too much—seemed like she was always out. She smiled at me like we was friends or something, with this mouth of straight white teeth, wearing clothes I'd wear to clean house in, but on her it didn't matter. She had blond hair like an angel (never saw one with black hair, which was something to think about), green eyes like emeralds, all these freckles.

Said she, "Well, hi there, Opal! I've come to the healing."

"I thought maybe you was on your way to the dump," I said, "except you all don't go to the dump yourselves."

She laughed like I was some TV comedian and said, "I brought a friend with me. He's parking the car."

Daddy and Mum and Bobby John were loading dishes and stuff from lunch into the van.

Mum called out, "That *you*, Sally?"

"It's me, Arnelle. I've come to the healing."

"Well praise the Lord and welcome!" Mum said.

"I got inspired by Doctor Pegler this morning, I guess."

Daddy said, "He's a fine man, praise the Lord," which was not the same thing Daddy said in the house, times he'd seen Guy Pegler on the TV. Then Daddy always said, "Can't beat that. Can't beat that," meaning he was into worrying again about people thinking they could go to church right in their own living room, instead of down to some real church.

Another thing that worried Daddy was folks who went to The Hand sending in their money to the TV preachers, instead of dropping it into the plate. Our offerings were way down, and Daddy said inflation was only half the problem.

"It ain't inflation," Daddy'd say, "it's infiltration. We are being slowly infiltrated by outsiders. They're coming right into the living rooms on the TV."

"Opal?" Mum said. "You better go on in and see if there's folks needing help. Old Mrs. Bunch is here on a walker from her rheumatism."

"Nice to see you, Opal," said. V. Chicken.

The wheels were already in motion. It was the start of things, but I didn't know that. I only knew I didn't like her being there, coming to sightsee at The Hand.

You could fill all the oceans in the world with what you don't know about your own beginnings and endings. In the movies music starts tinkling, telling you something's coming, telling you the mood is swinging you another way, warning you, preparing you, but in real life it just all comes down on you like an avalanche.

It'd been a year since we'd had a healing. Last time the healer was a short, tubby preacher from Newark, Ohio, who took sixty percent of the collection, that was his deal. We didn't make a hundred dollars because Daddy said he had all the charm and power of Bobby John. Daddy said he was just about as colorful as a sack of flour, and couldn't heal a cold sore in three weeks' time.

This Sunday we had K. Christian Keck from out of Philadelphia, Pennsylvania. He went fifty-fifty on the collection, had hair as red as the fires of hell, and was a crowd drawer so cars were parked as far back as the sign that said City Dump.

When I was little, I'd worry over who'd be healed and what if nobody was, but Daddy taught me there were very few miracles that happened right on the spot. He said we weren't to expect anyone to throw down their crutches or get up from their wheelchairs since healing was a slow process, whether the Lord was in charge or some doctor. Daddy said we only plant the healing seeds, and in His mysterious way God does the sprouting.

Daddy said sometimes Satan had fakes working for him, posing as men of God. He said they'd stage healings, put a well man in a wheelchair so's he'd jump right up after the laying on of hands, and claim he got healed.

"Oh, healings can happen real sudden in a service," Daddy said, "and we've seen it with our own eyes, but they always happen in Satan's services."

"Why?"

"They fake it so's they get a following. Word of mouth goes like a rabbit through a forest with his fur on fire. Pretty soon it's spread for miles and miles and Satan's man is said to have The Power. Folks will say, 'I saw him do it. I saw a lame man walk, he did it.' That's all you need."

Even though I'd been saved, I'd never really felt The Power, never got slain in the spirit, either.

There was something, though, I never talked about or told anyone, and that was my dream. I'd had the dream half a dozen times since I was little, always the same.

In it I was watching a speck, just a speck. Then in a light I could hardly look at, it was so bright, the speck would be coming into focus and getting bigger. I'd be trying to keep my eyes open against the terrible glare, to see what the speck was turning into. It'd grow and take a human form, and just before I had to shut my eyes against the brilliance of the light, I'd see myself, bigger than I was, as clear as though it was an enormous me inside a mirror. That was all. I'd wake up. I'd feel real, real good. I'd try to remember more. What was I wearing? Was I smiling? Was there something behind me? It'd all go, fall away, every detail, just when I'd almost see more. I'd lie there in the glow. There was only the glow for a while, and then the glow would go.

Who was I going to tell that to, anyway?

But that dream was mine, like a special secret I had, and if it had to do with the Lord, or the spirit, I didn't know.

I could feel the church starting to fill once I got into my seat. I got Mrs. Bunch on her walker up toward the front with me, and then I settled back. I shut my eyes awhile. I never liked to look around and try to gauge the crowd, because I hurt to see what was back there, the lame and blind, some sick in their minds so it showed in their eyes, those bent with afflictions, all of it.

I opened my eyes in time to see V. Chicken headed past my row to sit ahead of me two rows.

That was my first glimpse of him.

Once, in the cafeteria at Central High, six or seven of you come to where I was eating my peanut-butter sandwich and plunked yourselves down at the table.

There's not a one of you knows the way something sinks inside you when you're about to be picked on. The blood in your veins starts pulsing and you think they could see your heart jumping under your clothes like something small and alive caught under your sweater.

"Opal," one of you started in, "I hear down at your church you do something called talking in tongues."

I never said nothing back.

"Can you talk in tongues, Opal?"

"Let's hear it, Opal."

"Is it like this, Opal? Cook a look a book a dook a duck."

"No, it's more like blocket tockety tookety truck."

All getting into the act, laughing, speaking gibberish —do you remember that day?

Daddy told me that night, "They was just curious, Opal. Next time tell them calmly how we believe when certain people receive the Holy Spirit they find a mysterious language, described in I Corinthians XII tell 'em, the heavenly language of angels."

"That'd go over real big," said Bobby John. "Just keep your mouth shut, Opal. That's all you can do."

"Shush. Hush"—Mum. "They don't know anything down to that high school. Just tell them once your own mum thought the whole idea of tongues was funny as a chicken with its head off until the day she seen the light."

"Praise the Lord," said Daddy, who'd rather hear Mum do tongues than anyone at The Hand.

Even I got chills sometimes hearing her, after all this time.

"What neither of you understand," said Bobby John, "is that them high-school kids aren't interested in tongues, they're out to get you!"

"Then get them back!" Daddy shouted. "Don't come bellyaching to this supper table with your mum's best meat loaf spread before you, and all the blessings of the Lord your birthright! Don't come complaining of the tares when the Lord Jesus said wheat and tares will grow together, the good and the bad both at the same time! Get your eyes on wheat, not tares!"

"Okay, amen," said Bobby John. "I'm sorry, Mum."

"Daddy's had a hard day, too," she said

I muttered, "I'd like to know *how* to get them back."

"Speak up, Opal!"—Daddy.

"She said she'd like to know how to get them back," said Bobby John.

"A girl with a wasting disease, in a leg brace, came

to me today for no other reason than a simple blessing," said Daddy. "And you think you got troubles."

He could always top me.

Now about what I thought when I first laid eyes on
him.

At first I thought it was him. Bud.

I thought it was Bud back, looked so much like
him.

I wanted to die of shame seeing him see me there
in The Hand with all the sick.

I wanted to kill V. Chicken.

I remembered the sentence again, this time the
words sinking like lead in the center of my insides:
"Opal, you've got real pretty eyes, and someday—"

Then when I knew it wasn't Bud, what'd I think
next?

Not much.

On television sometimes they put someone under
hypnosis in the police stories, say now think back
very carefully: What happened, what exactly happened?

The way I saw him was the way I'd see him today,
his tiny hands so small for a boy, his lips always
wet-looking, his eyes glancing up at mine with that
soft, sweet look, his way of saying my name different
from how anyone else ever said it. He called me
Oh-pull, stretching it out, making it more.

I go back to then. He had on a blue shirt. I swear
his blue eyes were that bright that I could see their
color clearly, in the sunlight filtering through the
stained-glass windows Daddy still owed for.

We saw each other for the first time in a burst of
asthmatic coughing thundering out of Mrs. Turban,
who came up from The Hollow for the healing.

He looked around at her. She always sounded as
though she was gagging out her last breath. I saw his
hairline and the way his hair curled above his collar,
or I make that up.

I make it all up.

I don't remember anything about the first time I laid eyes on him.

I want it as a part of the mystery, but it isn't mine to have.

All that is mine about the moment is the sight of V. Chicken, and the sickness back inside me, wanting no part of The Hand, wanting to be anyone but Opal Ringer, embarrassed for myself, the speck of my dream that doesn't know about the glow coming.

And yes, the worst happened.

Sometimes you feel it building.

You don't—not in your churches. I've been to your churches. If anyone was to call out in the spirit in your churches, the usher'd hightail it down the aisle to find out what was wrong.

We called out.

I never did, but I've been listening to others call out since before my head came higher than the back of the pew in front of me.

"Oh Lord, thank you!"

"Yes, Jesus!"

"Yes my Lord Jesus!"

Call out, hold your palms up like you're feeling for rain. The Power comes in through the palms.

K. C. Keck was receiving those for healing up by the altar railing. People were filing up the aisle. The choir was singing softly: *"Some of these days I'm going home where no sorrow ever comes. . . ."*

When they come to the part that goes "And I'm gonna . . . sit down beside my Jesus . . . Lord, I'm gonna . . ." a man in the aisle began to stamp his feet and shout, "Hallelujah!"

Others shouted it, too. "HALLELUJAH!"

People were moving to the music. People were moving.

Beside me, Mrs. Bunch said, "It's starting, Jesus!"

Normally I was more pleased than anyone when it started; I was at least as pleased as anyone. Because it didn't always get off the ground. When it did, we

got happy, and the offering was always bigger, and
Daddy's face relaxed. . . . I'm coming to Mum.

A woman in the aisle purely screamed, "Yes! In
that house on the other side!"

Folks joined in. "I'm gonna shake hands with the
elders, Lord!"

Began shaking hands, everyone, with the ones in
front, in back, beside.

At the altar they were all laying hands on a woman
kneeling, and K. C. Keck had come forward, was
standing there before us with his eyes shut, his arms
in front of him, palms up, like he was ready to catch
something. He began shouting, "Someone is with us
today who feels The Spirit healing him or her. Someone is with us today who knows the Lord Jesus right
this minute is working a miracle! Someone *feels* it!
Someone wants to shout with joy!"

"Praise the Lord!" shouted from everywhere. Palms
up. Faces cut with smiles and lit up with the light.

I shut my eyes not to see V. Chicken and him,
after I saw them give each other these looks.

I opened my eyes to hear the shout: "The pain is
gone!"

"Praise the Lord"—everyone, turning to look behind them, and coming forward, carrying her crutch,
was none other than Diane-Young Cheek from Central High. My brother had been trying to get her
saved for months.

"I don't need it!" and she was shaking her crutch,
walking down the aisle with tears coming from the
center of a hurricane of hair.

"Praise the Lord!"—everyone.

Diane-Young Cheek kneeled down at the railing
while K. C. Keck kneeled with her, his arm drawing
Diane-Young to him, their eyes closed, Keck, praying.

Then Mum came away from the choir, and crossed
to the stairs and I knew what would happen next,
knew what V. Chicken and him would have to take
back to tell all of you.

I watched Mum go down the stairs, that certain

look on her face, blank eyed, smiling, carrying her head high.

Mum kneeled down with Keck, and Diane-Young Cheek, who was prone, slain in the spirit, spread out facedown on the altar rug like she'd been shot from behind.

The choir stopped singing.

The stillness moved in like heavy fog.

I felt my face get hot with shame, my heart going, waiting for her, hating them for being there and making me see Mum through their cold eyes, hating them for how my heart turned against my own around them.

Mum began.

"Theo lam day, theo ta tum, theo, theo ta tum, theo theo—" and Mum was straightening up while she did tongues, with the sun like an omen knifing through the stained-glass windows and pointing in her sweet face. Very slowly her big body began to sway.

People began calling out, "Oh yes! Yes!"

"Theo ta ta, theo ta ta—"

"Yes, Jesus! Yes!"

"Theo, theo," and Mum's feet began this slow-motion march, faster into a jerky little jig, until her steps grew wider, sweeping her around, almost like she was waltzing by herself.

She was dancing in the spirit, dancing away, struck by a music from deep inside of her, so powerful it didn't matter to her no more she was fat.

Four

JESSE PEGLER

One day Opal would ask me what I really thought of her the very first time I ever saw her.

Opal never asked you what you thought, she asked you what you really thought, as though she knew when you said what you thought, you always held something back.

I told her I thought she looked embarrassed because we'd come to the healing. ("Embarrassed?" she said. "Is that your name for it?")

I didn't tell her what I really thought when I first saw that little face peering at me.

That face reminded me of the face my grandmother made on pies before she'd bake them. She'd carve the eyes and nose and mouth into the dough, and there'd be this frightened-looking little white pie face.

She wouldn't make them smile and she wouldn't make them frown, because she said after all we had to eat them, didn't we?

Maybe Grandma didn't intend those pie faces to look so terrified, but they always looked to me like they knew we intended to devour them.

Something else, too, about the very first time I saw Opal.

When her mother went into tongues, I saw myself when I was four, sitting under the tent beside my folks, while my grandfather, Reverend Jesse Cannon, fell to his knees onstage, and cawed like a crow.

He'd finished leading us all in prayer before it happened, and once he got to his knees and made those noises, everyone around us was calling out, "Jee-sus! Praise the Lord!"

"What's happened to Grandpa?" I asked.

These sounds were sputtering out of him like blood from a fresh wound, and the eyes in his face were stark and watery like the breathless, pastel eyes of a fish at the end of a hook.

"He has tongues," my father said. "Shhhh."

And once I knew he intended what he was doing up there, my bones felt as though they were melting away in the intense heat of my own humiliation.

"He's raptured." My mother smiled down at me, and tried to take my hand, which I yanked away, wanting no part of her flesh and blood and weirdness.

I was flung back in time when I first saw Opal Ringer, suffering with her without her ever knowing it.

"Embarrassed?" she would say much later. "Is that your name for it?"

At the end of the service Seal grabbed my hand— hers was warm and wet—and she said excitedly, "Oh wow, Jesse!" whispering. "I never saw anything like that, did you?"

"Yes."

"Not like that," she said as though there could be no way I could have, and she began leading me down the aisle, hurrying, threading our way through the crowd.

I should have known I could count on Seal not to get scared or silly like some outsiders did their first time. Years ago when we were doing services under the tent, kids from nearby towns would come out on their bicycles to "see the show."

There was one song my grandmother sang that always cracked them up. It was called "I Come to the

Garden Alone." The line that got to them was ". . . *and the voice I hear, falling on my ear . . .*" They'd guffaw and nudge each other, pretend they were about to keel over, and hold their ears.

Other kids just beat it out of there, like their clothes were suddenly on fire, particularly when tongues started.

I remember bawling once when I was little, because I thought they were all watching us the way they'd watch a freak show. Bud said not to get into feeling sorry for myself; a lot of the stuff that went on under the tent *did* look bizarre to outsiders. Face it, we're bizarre, Bud said, but we've got good intentions and that's all that counts.

"I just wish we could have good intentions without being bizarre," I said.

"I just wish I was King of England," Bud said. "I just wish I was God Almighty. Don't waste your wishes. Take advantage of your advantages."

"You sound like Dad."

"Thanks. That's who I intend to sound like."

That was good old Bud, in the good old days.

"Seal," I said, as she pulled me along, "they're going to need a second healing if we keep knocking people around to get to the door."

Over her shoulder she said, "I want to get to her before she's surrounded," and yanked me more steps forward.

"Get to who?"

"Diane-Young Cheek." She stopped to whisper in my ear. "Better known as 'Why Die?' or 'Die Young.' She's the one who just got healed."

"What did she have wrong with her?" We were in motion again.

"She jumped out the gym window."

We were stopped by an old man leaving a pew, waiting for his wife to follow.

Seal said, "Just around the time Bud left, she took a dive right onto the pavement by the parking lot. She's lucky to be alive."

Down near the door, Diane-Young Cheek was sandwiched between Reverend Ringer and the healer.

I strained for a closer look at her, but a large
woman at the end of the aisle kept getting in my
way. All I could see of Diane-Young was this great
mop of curly, brown hair, attached to this long pole of
a body. She was carrying her crutch, a smile flicker-
ing and fading in the center of the mop, like a little
neon light blinking in a sign. I tried to imagine those
tiny eyes behind the pink lenses looking out a window
down at the pavement, panicked, like the faces I
always imagined went with the voices we often heard
over our Challenge hot line. *"I'm into dope and I
don't want to live anymore."* (Jesus wants you to
win. So do we.) "I'm going to take pills." (Before you
do another thing, will you pray with me?)

Just then the face of Opal Ringer came between
her face and mine for a few fleeting seconds. It was
the second time I saw her. She didn't see me. I saw
her tense profile. She was waiting to get out the
door, and I could see the anxious frown on her face. I
could sense how badly she wanted to get away from
there, and in that quick moment before she disap-
peared from sight, I felt like running after her, telling her I knew how it was.

I was taking all that in, the way you can in the
midst of a lot of other things feel some strange im-
pulse you don't act on, while other things are in motion.

Then I realized the large woman at the end of the
aisle was Opal Ringer's mother, the one who'd just
done tongues. People passing by her were thanking
her for dancing in the spirit, and she was nodding,
saying, "Oh, praise the Lord," but she was looking
straight at me.

I looked behind me and then back at her, and she
kept nodding, as if to say yes, it was me she was
waiting for. All smiles.

We came closer and she reached out for me. She
cried, "Bud! You've come home! Oh, thank Jesus!"

*   *   *

On the way home, Seal made me promise that I'd take Opal Ringer to something—a movie, a picnic at the beach, something special, Seal said, "So I can still look Arnelle in the eye after we get Diane-Young on *It's Up to You.*"

"We'll cross that bridge when we come to it," I said.

I remember Bud used to call her Seal Slavedriver sometimes, because she never gave up on an idea she got.

The afternoon we drove down to Central High to pick up Diane-Young and take her to meet my father, Seal slammed her elbow into my side.

"We've come to the bridge," she said. "There's Opal."

"I don't even know her," I complained.

"That's why I want you to introduce yourself," Seal said. "Now."

Five

OPAL RINGER

I guess when you've got money, you can do anything. I've known that to be true. How else would Diane-Young Cheek get herself transferred over to Central High, after she jumped out the gym window of Seaville High?

I remember her when she first showed up at Central, right in the middle of March, like doesn't everybody start new in a school in dead winter? Changing schools didn't stop the talk. But she was there one morning, limping down our halls on her crutch, just like anyone whose daddy owned CheckCheek Security, Inc., would go to Central.

She was this short, little, tough-talking tomboy, with wild brown hair that looked like big crows had made a nest on top of her head. Sitting on all that hair was a green cap, with CAT on it in gold, she wore with the peak in back. She had these bright-pink prescription glasses in silver frames, and silver braces all up and down her top and bottom teeth. She always wore corduroy Levi's and hooded sweat shirts, and big lace-up boots she called "shit kickers." She always had her radio/cassette over the opposite shoulder from the one with the crutch under it; top ten would blare from it and she'd chew gum in time with the music. You could always find her in the john, between classes, chain-smoking her More cigarettes, telling everyone to just call her D. Y. She said it to their backs because no one at Central knew what to make of her, much less what to say to her. She didn't fit anyone's picture of a rich kid, so some decided she was just a crazy, sent down to Central instead of off to Loony Tunes Hospital.

Her daddy pulled some strings to get her there, we all knew that. Maybe her daddy figured poor kids wouldn't be so mean, and she'd fit right in with us. What her daddy didn't know was kids are kids. Nice kids are nice kids and mean ones are mean ones, and someone like her was a target for anyone with Satan's meanness in his blood.

She was two grades ahead of me, so it was a while before I really met up with her. I might never have met up with her at all, if Bobby John hadn't taken to her, and spent most of what was left of his senior year being her protector. (The last girl Bobby John took up with was Selma Smetter, who was all the way in the other direction, a girlie girl who wore dresses all the time because she liked to, and used up all the school's toilet paper covering the seats good before she sat on them. She plugged her ears if she heard cussing, and sang solos at The Hand until she ran off with a bus driver bringing in Nassau County people for a healing. On her wedding day Bobby John got drunk the one and only time in his life, tore all her pictures in half, and put them in the garbage.)

Bobby John was the only one at Central, or anywhere else far as I knew, who ever called her D. Y. They took shop together, and she made him some kind of dumb-looking footstool he took to his bedroom and treated like it was treasure. He pulled it out from under his bed once a week, sprayed it with Pledge and polished it, and never put his feet on it.

Lunchtimes they ate together in the cafeteria. He'd trade her his Twinkies for her real chocolate éclairs from Fancyfoods. When she couldn't stand having her locker next to Ripper Blades', the school bully, Bobby John let her move her stuff into his locker.

Ripper Blades was one of the ringleaders of the group who called her names when she went by: Die Young Cheek was one name, Why Die?, Di-Dike, and Pink Eye.

She told Bobby John Central High was still better than Seaville, because she didn't really know the kids. She didn't have to walk in their direction when school was out, or ever meet up with any of them around Ocean Avenue where she lived. She said she never wanted to see the Seaville crowd again in her life, because she knew too much about all of them.

Bobby John said she didn't know about all of them, but she knew plenty about a lot of them, because her mother was the town shrink who specialized in teen-agers. Her mother called herself Dr. Antoinette Young, and she taped all her sessions with her patients. The thing that got Diane-Young into so much trouble was she sneaked down to her mother's office, listened to the tapes, and began telling stuff she'd heard about kids who went to Seaville. ("She had to do something," Bobby John said, "the way they was always picking on her.")

There was some kind of big showdown with the kids and their parents and Diane-Young's mother. Right after that, she drank a lot of Coca-Cola with rum in it and made her leap.

The first time I ever met her, really, was last winter. I came home from school and they were in Bobby John's room, off our kitchen. The phonograph was going, Gary S. Paxton singing "Jesus Keeps Takin' Me Higher and Higher."

I made a lot of noise getting myself some Flavor-Aid, and by the time I had the ice in it, they both came out to say hi.

She was on her crutch, and Bobby John had his arm around her neck. He was so much taller than she was, he couldn't get it around her waist without kneeling down next to her.

Bobby John's hair was all messed up from doing

something. Her hair always looked messed up, looked
like things might be making their home in it.

Bobby John was carrying this picture of Jesus Daddy
got for him. It was a neat picture because no matter
where you went in a room, His eyes followed you.

"This thing makes D. Y. nervous," Bobby John
told me, "so it's now all yours, Opal."

"It's the pits to have the eyes of Jesus watching
every move we make," Diane-Young said out of the
side of her mouth, "but it's so tacky I almost want to
keep it myself."

"I wouldn't call it 'tacky,' " said Bobby John.

"You"—she gave him a little punch in the stomach—
"wouldn't know the difference."

They were always giving each other these little
punches. She'd aim one up at his chin and go "Pow!"
He'd pretend to pound her head and go "Pow! Pow!
Pow!"

It was Diane-Young who told Bobby John he let
Daddy walk all over him, told him he ought to fight
back. But she never criticized him in a mean way like
Daddy did. She'd aim her crutch at him from across
the room like it was a rifle she was going to shoot him
with for saying "ain't," or "she don't," and he'd correct himself (got to correcting me, too, when I'd slip)
and say, "Sorry, D. Y., honeybunch." He got her to
stop saying "shit" every other word ("Excuse my
French, B. J.," was what she'd say), and both of
them found a lot of things real funny I never saw the
humor in. They'd laugh and laugh and tickle each
other all over.

They spent a lot of time in his room, when Mum
wasn't home, her radio/cassette playing top ten full
blast once she got tired of Gary S. Paxton, which was
about all Bobby John had for records. When Mum
was home, they'd hang out in Bobby John's car in our
backyard.

It was her bought him the CB radio Daddy never
let him forget he got from a woman.

"One thing I never did was take anything from a

woman," Daddy'd go around boasting, "particularly one who don't look like a woman, and for another thing ain't been saved."

Bobby John would say he was working on getting her saved, then slouch out to his car and fiddle with the CB: "Put your ears on, good buddy, and put the hammer in the toolbox. Make a 10-25 with the Lord Jesus Christ. If you don't, you're headed for a 10-70."

One afternoon last April I came home to find them sitting in the kitchen with this radio/cassette of hers on the table.

"Quiet, please, Opal," Bobby John said, "because we're trying to hear this tape D. Y. is playing."

"Praise the Lord," I said, dropping my books on the kitchen counter and hurrying to sit down and listen, because I thought now we were going to hear everyone's secrets, too.

What came out instead was Diane-Young's mother.

Di-Y, now that you feel so rejected by the Seaville High crowd, aren't you going too far in the other direction? If it was Reverend Cloward's son, Dickie, who you were seeing, we would welcome your interest in him, and your new religious enthusiasm. What we are not comfortable with is this Pentescostal religion, and we are not comfortable with this B. J. His background is too unlike your own. His particular faith is not for educated, sensitive people. It is a shouting, emotional mishmash based on superstition and mistaken, literal interpretation of the Bible. Di-Y, dear, religion is a quiet, inward questioning. Commotion isn't emotion. Fever isn't fervor. Deep, true, honest feelings never shout, dear. Now that I've shared my thoughts with you, tape yours to share with me. Remember, there is a u in us.

Diane-Young turned off the tape. "Well, you guys, that was my morning message yesterday, which is why I say life is such a shitty pity, pardon my French."

She said her mother often got up early, taped her a morning message, and left it on her napkin at the breakfast table before she went to her office.

Bobby John said, " 'O clap your hands, all ye people; *shout* unto God with the voice of triumph.' . . . It says that right in Psalms. Says 'all the sons of God *shouted* for joy.' Says *leap* for joy in Luke."

"Chester Best Cheek and Dr. Antoinette Young think emotionalism is crappy, Bobby John," Diane-Young said, "and kissing anyplace but at the airport, on the cheek, is the pits."

" 'Let him kiss me with the kisses of his mouth,' " Bobby John said. "Song of Solomon."

"Song of Solomon, but definitely not song of Chester Best and Dr. Antoinette," said Diane-Young.

"When The Rapture comes, everybody'll be kissing all over the place," I said, "and it'll be all right to do it."

"10-1. I don't have a clue what your sister's talking about," said Diane-Young, lighting up a More.

"I said when The Rapture comes *everybody*'ll be kissing—"

Bobby John didn't let me finish. "She's all taken up with The Rapture," he said.

"10-1," Diane-Young said. "10-1. What's The Rapture?"

"It's when we get lifted up to heaven without dying," I said, "and when it comes, everybody'll be—"

"Opal!" Bobby John barked at me. "Can't you see we got a serious problem here and we don't want no talk of The Rapture right this minute."

"I was just trying to make you feel better," I said.

Hot nights in summer sometimes I'd sit in my room in the dark and sing softly to myself, sing songs like

> *Somebody knows when your heart aches,*
> *And everything seems to go wrong,*
> *Somebody knows when the shadows*
> *Need chasing away with a song.*

I knew there was more in me waiting to burst out, bigger sounds caught way back in my heart, but I never bade them come forth.

When I was just about sung out, I'd put my radio on, and outside my window I'd hear you all going places in twos. Hear your cars and shouts.

Just like into the ark, in twos.

You'd go to your hangout, The Sweet Mouth Soda Shoppe, across from the A&P, and I'd wonder what you'd say in there for hours, what you'd do when the sodas were all drunk, sitting there in booths for half the night.

Daddy'd say, "Opal, I never want you to date anyone unsaved, hear?"

"Well, that isn't something I think you have to worry about, Daddy, since no one's pounding on the front door to get in for a date with me."

"The time will come," he said.

What used to get me in my heart of hearts was you all going by in your cars, some with tops down, tape decks playing, hair flying in the wind—I'd watch you without you knowing it.

I'd ask myself: If Jesus was to say you could be down there right now laughing your fool head off in The Sweet Mouth Soda Shoppe with the rest of them, or be a part of The Rapture, what would you choose? My answer'd come The Rapture, but I'd wrestle sons of Satan arriving at that conclusion.

Sometimes I hated being just a watcher.

I remember right after the healing, that last week of school, when we were cleaning out our lockers and taking tests. One afternoon when it was real hot, like August weather, V. Chicken showed up at Central High with Jesse, in her little sports car. Top down. Music playing.

I came out the front steps and it was the first thing I saw.

I was carrying my plastic book bag with "Let the Son Shine!" written on the sides. The handle was broken, so I was carrying it under my arm, and wished I wasn't when I saw her behind the wheel, because she'd be offering me one of her book bags next thing. ("Do you know anyone who can use this?"

was what she'd say, both of us knowing who could use it.)

Head down, I had no plan to even look in her direction, curious as I was to see what those two were doing down at Central. Then Jesse Pegler called out my name, loud as a blast on the ram's horn: "Oh-pull!" saying it the way he did. "Oh-pull!"

I'd have had to pretend I was stone deaf not to look around.

"Hi," I said, so soft only I could hear myself.

He just jumped right over the side of the car, not even opening the door to get out, and came loping across the green lawn up to where I was walking on the pavement. "Don't call me Bud, now," he said, putting his little hand across my mouth, grinning at me. "Your mother's already done that."

"I know."

"She tell you?"

"When you came to the healing that day. She thought you were Bud."

"I'm his brother, Jesse."

"I know."

You could smell they'd just cut the lawn, and there was a soft wind blowing in our faces, ruffling his hair.

"How are you?" He stood there smiling down at me.

"I don't know."

He bent double laughing at that one. "What kind of an answer is I don't know?"

"I'm all right." I didn't even know him yet, which was why it was hard.

"I suppose you know Bud?"

"I know him from working up at the von Hennig's, same as Mum."

"We're brothers," he said, so I knew he was real nervous himself.

Then out the front door of school Diane-Young came, in her green corduroy Levi's and red hooded sweat shirt, sweating hard in the heat, with her "shit kickers" on and her radio/cassette blaring out top ten.

"Diane-Young!" V. Chicken shouted. "Hey! Diane-Young!"

Diane-Young stopped in her tracks and looked around with this "Who, me?" face. She held a hand up to her pink glasses and looked toward the car.

"Yes, you!" V. Chicken shouted.

Diane-Young did one of her funny I May Faint numbers, holding her CAT cap on with one hand, staggering as though she was going to fall down from shock. She did that all the way to the car.

"We're taking Diane-Young over to meet my dad," Jesse said.

I didn't ask why, but I wanted to.

Jesse said, "Gee, Opal, we'd give you a ride, but the car's too small."

I could see Diane-Young getting into the jump seat, while V. Chicken held her radio/cassette for her. If Diane-Young saw me, she didn't let on.

"I always walk, anyways," I told Jesse, shifting my broken book bag from under one arm to under the other.

"I just wanted to introduce myself. We're both P.K.'s."

"What's P.K.'s?"

"Preachers' kids."

Even the horn on her car sounded different from other horns, sounded like some goose honking overhead.

Jesse called back that he'd be right with them.

Then he said, "I'll see you, Opal."

"All right," I said, but I didn't believe it. And there was Diane-Young, back in with them from up at Seaville High, laughing in the backseat, with the sun making all the silver in her mouth flash.

Jesse said, "Okay, Opal?"

Then ran off, almost as though something had been promised.

*　　*　　*

He got me thinking about Bud, I guess.

Maybe he got me thinking about him and I just thought I was thinking about Bud, but I didn't know enough about him like I did about Bud.

Before Bud ran off you couldn't be up to the von Hennigs' very long without being aware of Bud Pegler.

There was a case of a whole family, with the help included, being in love with one boy.

If he wasn't there in person, he was being talked about, or he was looking at you from out of a picture frame in her bedroom or her bathroom.

She'd pin his notes up on her cork bulletin board, too, for anyone to read, that's what amazes me.

Sweet passion, beloved baby, you blow away my mind.

One of them said that, and she just put a pin in it and stuck it up there next to a torn stub from Seaville Cinema, souvenir of some movie they'd seen together.

I'd've buried a note like that in my sock drawer if anyone'd sent it to me, which isn't a likelihood I'm going to lose any sleep over.

I think I lost a lot of sleep imagining being in her shoes, know I did. One time I put on one of her cashmere sweaters, then crossed my arms across my chest and felt the sleeves with my fingers, thinking of him holding her, and the softness he touched. Sometimes he began his notes: *Dear soft, green-eyed lover,* sometimes just *Seal, soft Seal.*

Seems in that house when he wasn't there it stopped breathing until he was. You'd hear Mrs. von Hennig call out, "What time's Bud coming by, honey?" Hear Seal's father telling her, "When Bud comes, I want to show him something, sweetheart."

Even the cook, who looked mean enough to star in a horror show, said she was making cinnamon rolls for Bud, or frosting a cake with coconut because Bud loved coconut.

In my time I've had daydreams and night dreams

of Bud. Then when he took off they stopped some until Jesse showed up in my life.

Then in some of my daydreams Jesse said everything Bud would say, which had to be the most secret part of my whole existence. No one even guessed, I know that much.

Afternoons after school I'd take my pillow off my bed, go sit in my chair looking out my window, thinking of summer coming with the pillow hugged against my body.

I'd think of the last week in July. I'd think of The Last Dance.

You would have all probably had a good laugh at the idea of Opal Ringer dreaming about going to that dumb dance of yours, but I was that human.

I'd seen V. Chicken dressing for it often enough, felt the excitement up there in their house those hot days of summer getting ready for the big event.

It is like you to have something called The Last Dance in the middle of summer, as though you really know no dance you dance will ever be the last one. There will always be another dance for you.

In my daydreams there was Jesse then, or Bud again, one of them crooking his arm out to touch my fingers to, holding on lightly, on my way with one of them to the lawn of St. Luke's Church, to The Ladies' Association of Seaville Township's big dance of the year. A summer's night, under the stars with the smell of honeysuckle from the bushes on the church grounds, moon coming up and me wearing my favorite color, which is lemon yellow.

Bud saying, "Opal, you've got real pretty eyes, and someday—"

Jesse saying, "We're P.K.'s, sweet passion, beloved baby."

The next time Diane-Young Cheek came into view was right across our living room on the fourteen-inch screen of our Sears Sensor Touch TV.

School'd been out a week, and I still didn't have a full-time summer job, just part-time stuff, helping out at the von Hennigs', waitressing here and there weekends.

This was on a Sunday, about a half hour after the noon whistle blew.

Mum was out in the kitchen cutting up carrots for a chicken-in-the-pot, in her own little world, humming, "Remember Whose Child You Are," barefoot.

Daddy was counting that morning's offering from The Hand over on the card table, while Bobby John read the comics.

Daddy, Bobby John, and I had finished watching Guy Pegler's sermon, which he called "Chopsticks."

He told how these folks went to a Chinese banquet, and when they took up their chopsticks to get at their meal, they couldn't reach the food in front of them because the chopsticks were too long.

The reason for that was everyone was supposed to feed the person across from them. "Feed each other in life!" Guy Pegler shouted out. "Give and you shall receive!"

It's Up to You was offering little gold chopsticks for charms that week, too.

Bobby John said he was waiting for the P.S., looking from the comics to the TV.

Bobby John said, "Not many people I know can even handle chopsticks."

"I wouldn't like to be waiting for any food you was going to be passing across the table to me on chopsticks," Daddy told him.

"You ever tried to pick up chop suey with them things?" said Bobby John.

"Well, it's a good sermon all the same," said Daddy. "You can't knock that sermon any."

"It's a good sermon if you're Chinese," said Bobby John.

"It's a good sermon," Daddy said.

Bobby John said, "You want me to help count up the offering?"

"This offering's not going to take two of us to count," said Daddy. "The cat could count this offering. . . . I think I'll go in my room to pray."

"Wait for the P.S., Daddy," said Bobby John. "Don't turn off the TV yet."

Mum shouted in to count the offering *after* dinner. "You're going to lose your appetite, Royal."

"Be better if we all lost our appetites with this slim an offering," said Daddy.

While The Challenge Choir sang "The World Needs a Melody," the camera showed their faces, then the ocean waves, then a gull flying with silver wings into blue clouds, then Guy Pegler in his royal-blue robes with his hands up, then back to the choir, the ocean, et cetera.

I was combing the cat when I heard Guy Pegler say ". . . a special guest in our P.S. segment from right here in Seaville."

The three of us looked up at that one, and that was when we saw Diane-Young Cheek standing there on the balcony with Guy Pegler's arm around her shoulders.

"You know your girl friend was going to be on?" Daddy asked Bobby John.

"I know something went to her head ever since the healing," Bobby John said.

Next thing we knew, Diane-Young Cheek was telling how Jesus Christ took her pain away.

"I'd gone to this place we have here called The Helping Hand Tabernacle," she was saying, and Daddy snapped, "This *church*."

"Well, we're getting a plug," Bobby John said. "At least we're getting that."

I called out to Mum that we was on national television. "Hurry and see!"

Guy Pegler said, "And what happened at The Helping Hand Tabernacle?"

"That's twice," Bobby John said.

Mum was in the room by then, paring knife in one hand, carrot in the other. "Praise the Lord!"

Diane-Young Cheek told how Reverend Keck and Reverend Ringer prayed over her.

"She's in the big time now," said Bobby John.

Guy Pegler said softly, "Diane-Young, I want to interrupt you long enough to tell our viewers you were in great pain because you'd tried to take your life."

Mum sucked in her breath and said, "Well, the dirty linen's out on the line now, for all to see."

"Satan's linen is never clean," Daddy said.

". . . and then I heard about this healing," Diane-Young said.

"I tell you I was surprised when she showed up," Mum said. "Wasn't you surprised, Bobby John?"

"Never know what she's going to do," said Bobby John.

"*I* was surprised," I said. "She said her folks said we were too emotional down at The Hand."

"I expect they're singing themselves some other tune now," Mum said.

"Keep quiet and listen," Daddy said.

". . . suddenly the pain was gone and I just fell over," Diane-Young said.

Mum said, "She was slain in the spirit. She fell in the spirit."

"Diane-Young, I want to thank you for appearing with me this morning, and helping others realize that Jesus wants you to win!" Closeup of Dr. Pegler. "So do I!"

Then The Challenge Choir began singing, *"Run, climb, reach for a star!"*

Daddy said, "Well, we got something to give thanks for here, seems to me."

We bowed our heads while Daddy said a prayer of Thanksgiving.

The prayer began, "O Lord, help us keep humble," and no sooner ended when Bobby John began pacing around saying he supposed it was a good thing, he supposed a nationwide plug was a good thing.

"You should praise Jesus, son," Mum said. "You helped bring her to Him."

"Well, I was her mintor all right."

"You was her *mentor*," said Daddy. "You wasn't her mintor. Sounds like you was in charge of her breath. Mintor."

Later that day I got up from a nap, and the whole house was quiet except for Bobby John whispering into the phone. He'd pulled the cord into the living room, and was crouched over on the living-room couch.

"You could have told me you was going to be on nationwide TV, D. Y. . . . Now, that ain't the point. It isn't the point. It isn't that we want anything, honeybunch. I just miss you so."

He stopped talking when he saw me and said, "Opal's in the room now."

I started to leave when he said, "Opal, wait." Then into the phone, "I'll ask her. But you remember what I said."

He put his hand across the mouthpiece and said, "Opal? The Cheeks are having a dinner party for Dr. Pegler and his wife and Jesse. They want you up there next Saturday night."

In those few seconds before I answered, I saw Jesse's face, Bud's, smelled the honeysuckle at St. Luke's, crazy, jumbled pictures in my head, until I finally managed to say, "What they want me for?"

"To help serve," Bobby John said, as though I ought to know that as well as I knew my own name.

Something else . . . When Daddy woke up from his nap, Bobby John announced the Cheeks were going to put in a whole new CheckCheek Security System at The Hand. He had this big grin on his face. "It's free from them to us, Daddy."

"What for?" Daddy said.

"In gratitude for D. Y.'s healing, Daddy."

"The Hand's never been locked since it opened," Daddy said.

"There's been some stealing going on in The Hollow, Daddy. People been taking things from houses."

"Taking things?" Daddy said. "The Lord commanded us if any man take your coat, give him your cloak besides, or don't you remember your Bible?"

"They just thought—"

"They just didn't think," said Daddy. "We don't need no CheckCheek Security in our Savior's church, thank you all the same."

Six

JESSE PEGLER

The night we were going to dinner at the Cheeks',
my mother said the Cheeks were "very important."

I could just hear Bud's voice saying, "Oooh, they
must be filthy rich!" . . . Then my father answering
him, "Rich as Croesus, right you are, and fund raising for the Lord happens to be every bit as important
as annointing the sick or feeding the starved!" Bud
would have piped up well, it was good my father felt
that way because we did a lot more fund raising than
we did annointing or feeding. . . . It was one of their
old running arguments.

Me—I just bitched a lot and ended up showering
and changing into my best clothes.

My father came by my room as I was finishing
dressing.

He was wearing a new dark-blue thin-pinstripe
suit, a light-blue shirt, and an ACE tie. The tie was
patterned after a club tie, only instead of heraldic
devices or sporting symbols, "ACE" was repeated
across it in tiny gold letters against a blue background.

"Jesse," my father began, "one thing experience
has taught me is—"

I braced myself for some lesson in morality or
philosophy, but he continued, "—that a narrow tie
width is better on men our size. Bud can get away

with a fatter tie with his height, but we're not blessed with six-foot frames."

I remembered my father when he'd buy ties by the half dozen in a serve-yourself drugstore, only making sure they weren't all the same color.

"I don't have anything narrower," I said.

"You may borrow one of mine," he said. "One of my paisleys would look good with what you have on."

"Okay," I said. I reached up and began undoing my tie. "How come you have on a blue shirt?" I asked. "We're not being televised tonight, are we?"

He always wore blue on the tube, to match his eyes.

"You'll see the reason for that later. It's a surprise," he said. He said that Donald Divine, the ACE public relations man, was waiting for them downstairs in his study.

"When you've finished up here, stop in and say hello to Donald, okay, Jesse?"

"Yeah," I said.

"We're due at the Cheeks' at seven-thirty. . . . And Jesse," he said, "I don't insist on this, but I was always touched when my boys would answer yes, sir, instead of yeah or okay."

"Yes, sir," I managed.

He slapped my back and said, "I love you, son!"

"I love you, too, *sir*."

We both laughed at that. Then he went bounding out of the room and down the stairs—Bud liked to say he was born with his motor running. I think they both were.

I went into my parents' room and got one of my father's ties. Then I just stood there looking around at all the photographs of our family. They were everywhere: on the wall, in little frames set out on top of the bureau, even some stuck into the mirror on my mother's dressing table.

We were a pretty seedy-looking bunch in the days when Bud and I were little. My dad always seemed to be wearing a vest with his shirt sleeves rolled up.

My mom was usually in some flowered dress with a hat on, even in the hottest weather. Her hair wasn't as blond in those days, more brown than the bright yellow she'd changed it to.

In those days my mom couldn't afford manicures or hairdressers, and her dresses came off the racks at shopping-center stores.

Our tent, in the photographs, was usually somewhere in the background. Bud was always mugging for the camera, making faces or holding up two fingers behind my head, and my socks were always falling down. I was in clothes too big for me, Bud's hand-me-downs.

Seedy-looking as we were, we were all smiles, all of us.

In the later snapshots, particularly after Bud'd split, my father didn't smile. My mother smiled on cue from years of practice, but my father's emotions always went right to his face, so sometimes my mother had to remind him to leave his burdens behind while he faced people who might have greater ones.

My father's face in one recent photograph, stuck into a corner of my mother's mirror, looked like someone had socked him in the stomach. It was taken at the ground-breaking ceremony for The Summer House, just after Bud left. I was on one side and my mother was on the other. Donald Divine took the shot, and I remember my father'd just finished saying, "It's just a shame one of our number is missing."

He'd said that about a dozen times that day.

I wondered why he couldn't remember his battles with Bud, times he'd tell Bud he was sick of the sound of Bud's voice. One of their biggest battles was over the "prayer rugs" idea my father came up with in one of his brainstorming sessions with Donald Divine.

Supposedly, strips of our old canvas tent were to be sold for $100 apiece as prayer rugs. Smaller, wallet-size pieces were to go for $10. My father was to get up and announce that the tent was saturated and impregnated with The Power. "The power of the Lord had to pass right through the canvas, and now you can have a share of it."

Bud didn't like the whole idea to begin with, but when he found out the strips of canvas weren't even to be strips of the tent, he blew up. He said it was the phoniest pitch he'd ever heard about, and he called my father a con artist.

"Bud, Bud, Bud," my father began crooning back at him, "there's no way to get the canvas from our tent clean. Why, it's filthy!"

"Then don't say it's canvas from our tent! Don't say it has The Power in it!"

"But"—my father's voice with a sharp little edge to it—"it's symbolic, not literal. Why, if it was literal we wouldn't have enough to go around. We couldn't even make the offer."

"It's dishonest!" Bud shouting. "It's greasy!"

"I love you, Bud, but you're going too far now, young man!"

"It's a cheap trick!"

"I wonder, Bud, if you know how sick I am of hearing you mouth off!"

That was the only one of their fights that came to blows.

I don't know who hit who first, but Bud stumbled over a chair on his way out of the living room, cursing and holding his eye with one hand. My father's face was scarlet. He was breathing as though he'd run the mile, and his eyeglasses had been knocked to the floor.

Shortly after that, Bud took off.

The strips of canvas went like cold drinks on a hot summer's day. My father said they alone paid for a whole floor of The Summer House.

Still, on ground-breaking day, it was Bud causing my father's long face, and Bud my father was missing and mooning over.

I tried to make him feel better by telling him I missed Bud, too.

"You don't even know how it pains me, Jesse," he said, as though he had a knife in him and I'd scratched my elbow.

"Guy." My mther spoke up softly, almost a whisper, which meant she was about to deliver a necessary but not necessarily welcome truth. "We all miss Bud."

"Bud and I had a very special relationship," he said.

"We're sympathetic to that, Guy," said my mother, "but you have to share your missing him with others who miss him, too. When you can't do that, we've got two people to miss, Bud and you."

My mother could always nail it right to the wall, with one blow.

"Hello, Jesse." Donald Divine stuck out his hand and caught mine in a crushing blow. "Your dad has come up with another real winner."

He pointed to a poster leaning against my father's desk.

My father was finishing a martini.

While we stood there admiring the latest Challenge poster, I remembered back when my father was Brother Pegler, and he used to drop worms into tumblers of gin to show how lethal liquor was, that it killed worms instantly. (It was an old trick he'd copied from a famous evangelist named Billy Sunday.)

Bud used to tease him about it, say that it only showed people how to get rid of worms. "You'll have people all over the country saying they're only drinking to kill worms."

Dad was a teetotaler in those days.

The change came around the time Dad hooked up with Donald Divine. Most changes in our life came around that time.

The new Challenge poster was enormous. Printed across it was a giant-sized charge plate.

"Your dad's going to kick off our early summer

shows with a little gold charge plate charm," Donald said.

"How about another Martin?" my father asked him and, not needing to wait for an answer, scooped up Donald's glass along with his own.

I flinched at "Martin" for martini. My dad'd got that one from Igor Sonnebend, this rich Born-Again Christian, along with several thousand dollars for our Summer House building campaign.

Dad got along with Igor real well, but my mother said Igor Sonnebend made her uncomfortable, because there never seemed to be enough of anything for him in this world. He wanted more homes, more cars, more fine furniture . . . more more more. She said she'd rather see Dad back preaching under a tent that dependent on Igor for anything. They had a few arguments over Igor, because my mother said when a man like that kept getting so much, wasn't someone somewhere having to do with less?

My father insisted that Igor kept the wheels turning, that his needs kept people producing, kept people employed, but I don't think he ever convinced my mother of it. She said there ought to be an "enough" for everyone.

While my father was off in the kitchen getting more martinis, I stood with Donald and studied the poster.

CHARGE IT TO THE LORD!
"If he hath wronged thee, or oweth thee
ought, put that on mine account."
Philemon 18

It was times like that when I missed Bud most. I could see us up in our room, doubling over, holding our stomachs laughing. "A charge plate! . . . I—don't—be—lieve—it!"

Donald Divine always gave my father credit for every idea, but some of them were pure Donald. There was no way my father could have come up with some of them.

Bud and I called Donald "Divine Donald," and an idea like the charge plate, in the good old days, would have left Bud and me breathless from laughing, tears running down our cheeks. I sometimes think it was Seal who changed Bud, fired up his conscience so he got mad more than he laughed.

Donald Divine said, "Jesse, next Sunday is going to be a bang-up show."

Donald always called our services "shows."

He looked younger than his thirty-five years. He was the type who wore expensive tweed jackets with suede elbow patches, silk scarves, and tinted glasses. He blow dried his hair and had it cut regularly by a New York City stylist.

"It's your father's idea to do our show at sunrise from now on," said Donald.

My father was back in the room with martinis and a slab of Brie on a silver tray, surrounded by Carr's Table Water Crackers. ("Don't buy any crackers but Carr's," my father'd told my mother a while ago. "That seems to be the 'in' cracker.")

"Jesse," my father said, "can you figure out why we're switching to sunrise? I bet Bud could."

"Too bad he's not around to ask," I said.

My father made one of his pained little facial flinches and went right on. "Summers out here, people are heading for the beach," he said, "or they're house hunting or looking for next summer's rentals. We're dealing with a resort area here. Now, if we try to complete with that, ACE is going to get blamed for the traffic jams."

Donald said, "They're already three deep on the Montauk Highway by nine in the morning. We have a problem, anyway, but at least this early we'll cut it in half."

"Who's going to watch us at sunrise?" I said.

"We're going to tape the sunrise show and run it at our regular time," said Donald.

Then my father said, "Well, Jesse, have you noticed anything new?"

"It's a good poster," I managed.

"Not the poster," said my father. "Me, Jesse. Me."

Donald chuckled. "It proves my theory that kids don't notice their parents or what they do, until it affects *them*."

"I like to tell a story I once heard about John Denver, the singer," said my father, who liked to tell that story so well Donald and I had both heard it a few times already. "He took his boy for the very first time to one of his concerts. They went to the spot by helicopter. Now this youngster didn't really have any idea how famous his father was. As they were passing over the area where John Denver was to perform, they looked down and saw great masses of people waiting to get in, traffic jammed on all the highways. Well, the boy's eyes got big as saucers. He looked up at his daddy, John Denver, and he said, 'All these people came here to see some guy's dad get up and sing?' "

Donald slapped his knee and howled at the joke as though it was the first time he'd ever heard it.

I said, "What didn't I notice?"

"You asked me why I was wearing the blue shirt, and I told you I had a surprise," said my father.

Then I noticed.

Some guy's dad had on a new pair of trendy blue-tinted prescription glasses, replacing the old owl ones.

They were the same kind Donald wore.

It used to be you could always see and hear us coming. My dad drove this old beat-up van painted gold with BROTHER PEGLER in black letters on both sides. There were speakers attached to the roof, and tapes of songs like "We're Marching to Zion" to play through them.

Lately we drove around in a new dark-brown Cadillac Seville. In tiny gold letters on the door of the driver's side, there were just the initials ACE.

Before we went anywhere to fund raise, Donald always prepared a profile of our hosts. Even though we were supposed to be having a friendly dinner with the Cheeks that Saturday night, Donald had done a profile on them.

My mother read it aloud on our way there, while she sat up in front next to my father, and I sat in the back seat.

- Chester Cheek is the president of CHECK CHEEK SECURITY SYSTEMS, INC., a self-made multimillionaire.

- Dr. Antoinette Young Cheek is one of these modern "therapists" whose Ph.D. is in music, not psychology. She has an extensive local practice, with many clients who are teenagers from "the better families" in Seaville.

- She is an aggressive influence, skeptical about religious fund raising. (If the subject comes up, remember that a fifth of Christ's teachings was taken up with stewardship. St. Paul felt it was just as spiritual to discuss money as it was the Resurrection. Et cetera.)

- She is the power behind the throne. . . . He is more business-oriented, and has always been a philanthropist on a grand scale, but has never included religious organizations in his gratuities, except for a small amount yearly to First Methodist. They are members but infrequently attend services.

- Their only child, Diane-Young Cheek, is a somewhat troubled teenager who has been in and out of a series of private and public schools.

- Diane-Young is the reason they now make their home in Seaville—an attempt to raise her in a small-town environment. She is their weak spot, fairly friendless, and of a sly nature with a

suicide attempt in her background. She is highly
suggestible, which probably facilitated her
healing.

- Her mother is a balletomane. He is a member
  of A.A., and no liquor is ever served in their
  home.

At the last sentence, my father reached in his
pocket for his Breathbrace and gave his mouth a
spray.

"Guy, don't drive with one hand," said my mother.

"We're not exactly fighting our way through traffic."

Our car was the only one on the road leading down
to the ocean.

"There's a fog, though," said my mother.

I said, "What's a balletomane?"

"Donald says it's someone interested in ballet,"
said my mother. "Guy, you shouldn't wear those blue
glasses when you drive at night."

"I can *see*, Rhoda."

"How many martinis did you have, too?"

"I had one with Donald, do you mind?"

"I never mind if you take a glass of wine. After all,
Jesus turned water into wine, but he didn't turn it
into gin and vermouth. There's the turn," my mother
said. "This is their driveway. Did *you* know St. Paul
said it was just as spiritual to discuss money as the
Resurrection?"

"It's all through the New Testament," my father
said.

A good three minutes later we were there in front
of the Cheeks' house—the driveway leading up to it
was that long.

"Igor Sonnebend doesn't have anything on the
Cheeks," my mother said. "You could put his Palm
Beach house right down inside this one."

"Igor could have a house like this if he wanted it.
He's just not ostentatious."

"Wait a minute," my mother said. "I must be losing

my hearing. Did you just say that Igor Sonnebend wasn't ostentatious?"

I said, "That's what he said."

"Dog pile on the rabbit," my father said. "I'll never understand what you two have against Igor."

"I wouldn't call him a rabbit," my mother said.

Then she peered out the window at the Cheeks' house. "Look at this place! This is like Buckingham Palace!"

Wispy glimpses of an enormous stone structure loomed before us like a mountain behind the fog.

"Check my breath, please, Mother," said my father.

He blew at her and she said, "You're awfully minty."

Then we got out of the car and let the Cheeks' valet park it.

You could hear the ocean waves crashing down on the beach, out in back of the house. You could smell and feel the salt spray.

"Don't try and talk about ballet, because you don't know anything about it," my mother said.

"Who's going to try and talk about ballet?" I said.

She said, "I'm talking to your father."

"Who's going to try and talk about ballet?" my father said.

"Oh, we have a parrot along with us this evening," my mother said. My mother always made her little jokes when she was getting nervous.

"Who's going to try and talk about ballet?" I said.

"Who's going to try and talk about ballet?" my father said.

The truth was we were all getting nervous.

"Hush!" my mother whispered, giggling. "You two behave yourselves now."

At the top of long stone steps, in the light of the open door, a butler was waiting, with a maid behind him to take our coats.

"Good evening," the butler said. "My name is Grayson. The Cheeks want to thank you for not smoking."

"We don't any of us smoke," said my mother.

When we were out of earshot of Grayson, my fa-

ther said softly to my mother,"Don't explain yourself
to the help, Rhoda."

"He explained something to me and I explained
something back."

Coming from a far distance down a long hall, under
a gigantic crystal chandelier, a tiny woman approached.

My father, out of the side of his mouth, to my
mother: "Don't explain anything back to the help. It
isn't done."

"The Peglers!" the tiny woman called out on her
way to us.

My mother had on her best smile, but she looked
my father in the eye and murmured, "Guy Pegler, I
knew you when you were wearing white Sears, Roe-
buck socks with brown suits and black shoes, so get
down off your high horse, hear me?"

"Mrs. Cheek!" my father purred, bowed, smiled
ear to ear. "It's a pleasure to introduce you to my
family."

Seven

OPAL RINGER

Sometimes I don't understand the rules in this life, I swear before the Almighty.

Take the night I was hired to help serve over to the Cheeks'. I understood why I had to wear the hairnet, and the black uniform one size too big for me, with the crisp little white apron over it—I don't mean those rules. I mean ways of acting, like what you all did when I came through the kitchen door with the bowl of Brussels sprouts.

Sometimes a prayer is like a daydream that you say aloud to Jesus. Sometimes I prayed that when The Rapture came and I had my own tableful of guests, I'd say to whoever it was come through my kitchen door carrying the vegetable, "How you doing, honey? Put the plate down and pull the chair up, and dig in, darling!"

What you all did was pretend I didn't come through the door with the sprouts, and when you finally had to take them from me because there I was at your elbows, anything you said to me you said in little whispers, not looking at me.

V. Chicken was there and Jesse. Diane-Young. The Reverend Cloward with his wife and Dickie, and Dickie's sister, Verna. The Peglers and the Cheeks. And me, slowly circling the room with the vegetable, wondering what kind of crack in the sky would come if anyone had said out loud, "Hi, Opal."

Mrs. Cheek, who looked like a little bug in glasses, was talking to Guy Pegler when I got to her. "What Chester and I aren't comfortable with is all this endless money raising," she was saying, "and the TV preachers are the worst offenders, though I'm not criticizing you in particular." Whispered at me, almost in the same breath, "Opal. Thank you."

I had a mind to say what Mum said sometimes when she was feeling good and I started a sentence with "Mum." She grabbed me and cooed, "That's my name and lovin's my game," hugging me to her.

Dr. Pegler said, "You know, Mrs. Cheek—" then, "Dr. Young—"

"Antoinette. Please."

"Antoinette. A fifth of Christ's teachings was taken up with money and stewardship."

Mrs. Pegler said. "St. Paul considered it just as spiritual to discuss finances as he did to discuss the Resurrection."

By that time I was all the way around to Diane-Young, who didn't look like herself anymore. Bobby John had told me her hair got cut off, said Samson lost his strength that way. I said she's not a man, one, and two she was never known for her strength, so don't be so upset, Bobby John. But Bobby John was, whatever'd come between them since the healing.

With most of her hair gone, Diane-Young looked like a shaved dog in summer, or a plucked chicken. It was the first time I'd ever seen her when she didn't have on a hooded sweat shirt. She had this long skinny neck sticking out of this pink dress, the color of her glasses. Her little eyes darted up to meet mine when I served her the sprouts, and there was a fast flash of silver as she tried to smile.

She polished off the Brussels sprouts and I was headed back to the kitchen while Dr. Pegler was saying, "Do you remember your New Testament? One of the basic teachings is the importance of giving money to the Lord's work. Now, television eats money like a horse eats hay, but—"

Ripper Blades' mother was the other person hired to help out that night. She was talking to the cook as I walked into the kitchen.

"Well, at least she's walking without the crutch," she was saying.

The cook said, "That little girl did that before any healing." Then she saw me. "No offense meant where The Hand's concerned," she said.

"No offense taken," I said.

"Opal," she said, "don't touch the Crabmeat Imperiale. There's a tuna-fish casserole for us. We don't repeat what we see, hear, or say up here, Opal Ringer."

"Yes, ma'am."

I sat over on the stool and watched what was playing on the tiny TV on the counter, an old movie called *Voyage to a Prehistoric Planet.*

A cosmonaut was saying, "There's no fair or unfair to a meteorite. You get hit—you die."

I got to wondering again what death was, anyway, and if there really was a Satan's hell, or was it all words and no one really knew anything, just made things up.

Like Bobby John before I left the house, trying to come up with this snazzy sermon for Daddy. "Daddy," he said, "listen here, something interesting I come up with for you. You can use it if you want to. 'Success' is spelled with seven letters. Of the seven, only one is found in 'fame' and one in 'money,' but three are found in 'happiness.' "

Daddy just looked across the table at him like he was some ant dared speak out from the top of the anthill.

"Bobby John," Daddy said, "In the first place half the people come down to The Hand can't spell *period*. In the second place, no spelling lesson's going to pull them out of their living rooms where the TV's on. They're getting choirs of fifty and more in living color with all outdoors as a backdrop, and a preacher's had his hair done down to the beauty parlor, and you're going to give them a spelling lesson!"

"Well, I tried, Daddy."

"Yeah, well, tried has got an r, and an i, and an e in it, and so does failure."

The cook said, "You weren't invited up here to watch television, Opal."

"I'm not even watching," I told her.

"What do you call what you're doing?"

I thought of telling her I was wondering if there was a hell we'd all burn up in, and if there was how come we'd be able to burn without our bodies, which were somewhere back six foot under?

I shrugged my shoulders instead, and she said, "Go back in there with more Brussels sprouts, dear."

"You go to school with my son, Albert, don't you, Opal?"

"Yes, ma'am." Ripper Blades, pick on you after you were run over by a bus, he was so mean.

I took the bowl of Brussels sprouts and pushed through the swinging doors.

The Shadow, making a comeback.

Mr. Cheek was talking. He was this thin little man in a bow tie, with glasses so thick you couldn't see his eyes. "At first we weren't too comfortable with Di-Y's interest in religion."

"It wasn't religion per se," said Mrs. Cheek.

"It was this Pentecost—" and he glanced up at me, stopped himself in midsentence.

"You see," said Mrs. Cheek, "we don't express emotion very openly in this family."

"I know what you're saying," Dr. Pegler said.

Mrs. Pegler said, "The sound and the fury."

"Exactly," said Mrs. Cheek. "I like to say that commotion isn't emotion."

"Fever"—Mr. Cheek leaned forward—"isn't fervor."

"True feelings"—Mrs. Cheek leaned forward—"never shout."

"Exactly!"

"Exactly!"

"Opal?" Mrs. Cheek whispered up at me. "It's too soon to pass the vegetable again, thank you."

Even the cook there had her rules, told me one thing she made a rule was never to help with the cleanup. I was finishing drying the silver she said never went in the dishwasher, not real sterling. I was asking myself, if Jesus was to say you could eat off real china plates with real sterling silver utensils or be part of The Rapture, what would you choose?

"So you help Mrs. Blades, dear. I put the rest of the tuna-fish casserole in a Baggie for you to take home."

"Thank you, ma'am." I was watching the moon come through the fog in the sky out the window, wondering if heaven had a night. Never heard it had one. Heard it was paved with gold and shining without the need of the sun. Never heard hell had a day, only the light of the fires down there.

Mrs. Blades said, "Now you're leaving this little girl to help someone with a frozen shoulder."

"Someone with a frozen shoulder shouldn't hire out to do kitchen work," said the cook.

"This little girl's left to lift that big garbage bag and put it out in the can," said Mrs. Blades, but the cook, in her coat, was on her way out the door.

"You ought to come to one of our healings," I said, "and have them lay hands on that shoulder."

"I'm a Catholic, honey," she said. "I'm going to the chiropractor."

The last thing I did was haul the bag across the floor, through the back door. The air smelled fresh, like after a rain. A big, round moon had broken through the passing clouds, and I looked up at it, setting the bag down to catch my breath. I looked for shapes in clouds that could be omens, like Elijah's servant seeing the cloud rise from the sea like a man's hand, before the heavens turned black and the rain came.

"Psssst! Opal!" a voice said. "Over here!"

It was Diane-Young, standing in the shadows smoking a More.

'I've been waiting for Mrs. Blades to leave so I could talk to you," she said.

She put out the cigarette and helped me drag the Tidy-Tall to the can and lift it inside. "How's B. J. doing?" she asked me.

"He's dragging his tail some."

"Is that all he knows how to do? Ask him if that's all he knows how to do!"

"Did you and him have a fight?"

"Chester Best and Dr. Antoinette think I'm too much under his influence," she said. "They say I've got to raise my sights. They made me get this crappy haircut, too. Seal von Hennig gave them the idea."

"What's she care about your hair?"

"She's talking about ACE sending me out on a Winning Rally, to tell about my healing. She said I should get contact lenses and removable braces. I want you to tell B. J. something for me."

"He's coming to pick me up, in half an hour."

"They're watching me like a hawk," she said, "that's the shitty pity. But you tell B. J. I said 10-3."

"10-3?"

"10-3," she said and we heard the back door slam shut.

We heard, "Di-Y? Di-Y, are you out here, dearest?"

"I'm just helping Opal with the garbage, Mother."

"Why, how very thoughtful of you, Di-Y," said Mrs. Cheek, coming down the path toward us in her long green dress. "Opal, did cook pay you? Did she offer you a ride home?"

"Yes, ma'am, I'm paid, thank you. Someone's coming to get me if his car makes it."

"Di-Y," said Mrs. Cheek, "your friends are all gathered in the solarium. Why don't you take Opal in

there, and when her ride comes Grayson will tell
her."

"They're not my friends," said Diane-Young.

"They *are* your guests though, dearest," said Mrs.
Cheek.

Mrs. Cheek followed us inside and down a long hall
to the solarium, so we couldn't talk about Bobby John
anymore.

She said "the adults" were going to watch a film of
Rudolph Nureyev in *Swan Lake*.

What the Cheeks called the solarium was a long,
glassed-in porch at the back of the big house, with
these shiny black tiles and clean white rugs, black-
and-white cushions covering all the furniture, and
green, spidery plants hanging down from the ceiling.

"Everybody here knows Opal Ringer, don't they?"
Diane-Young said when we walked in.

"Opal!" V. Chicken gushed at me, just as though
I'd never passed her the Brussels sprouts earlier.
She was sitting on the couch with redheaded, freckle-
faced Dickie Cloward, who stood up and said he'd
met me at the First Methodist Church Strawberry
Festival last year. I remembered that thing real well,
because Daddy'd sat there on a folding chair going
300 X $3.25 comes to $975, and Mum said it was more
like 200 there. Well, we was late, Daddy'd said, must
have been a hundred here before we drove up. I'd
complained we didn't even get to enjoy anything anymore, because we were always counting up the take,
ours and everyone else's. Daddy'd told me we'd stop
counting up the take just as soon as my rich uncle got
out of the poorhouse.

Verna Cloward, who looked just like Dickie, smiled
real sweet at me, and next thing I knew Jesse Pegler
was on his feet, coming across to say, "Oh-pull! Sit
with me. We were just talking about my brother."

Verna Cloward said, "I was telling everyone that
my father says Bud's suffering from P.K.S. That's
Preacher's Kid Syndrome."

" 'Syndrome' is Dr. Antoinette Young's very favorite word," said Diane-Young. "She couldn't get to sleep at night if she didn't get to say 'syndrome' a dozen times every day."

"My father says," Verna Cloward continued, "that preachers' kids, particularly boys, have to go through a rebellious stage."

"What do you think, Opal?" Jesse said.

I shrugged, an inch from being stuck and I knew it. Mum said all you had to do when you got stuck was ask a question, let someone else do the talking, and Daddy said stuck was normal for a woman because they were supposed to listen anyway. " 'Let the woman learn in silence with all subjection,' " Daddy said. "One Timothy."

The window was open and waves slapped the beach in the distance. I had on a green sweater, acrylic, hole under the right arm. Mum said why wear the one with the hole, when you got the pretty red one to wear up there, the real wool one? I said because you-know-who's going to be up there, and if I run into her wearing it, how'm I going to feel in her old sweater? Mum said she didn't give it to you to put in your bureau drawer, she give it to you to put on your back. You don't know anything, I said. You just don't know anything.

I could feel the crazy blanket starting to come over my head, covering me like deep snows do rusty things left out on the lawn from fall when you took in other stuff.

Their conversation went on without me, after a few more attempts Jesse made to pull me into it.

Those of you who saw me that way got real uncomfortable—that I always knew from watching your faces, glances you gave each other, silences you left for me to fill, and when I wouldn't, wanted to die of your own embarrassment for me.

Soon I didn't even move, didn't even cross my legs or run my hand along my arm, or smile when you all smiled, to show I could still hear. I stayed statue still. I knew that I was there like some red, ugly

pimple on the side of someone's face, coming to a
whitehead in plain view, mortifying everybody.

I sat there while they talked of Bud.

Seemed like the world was in love with Bud. Gone
for so long, he was back all the time as big as when
he was really there. I could see him clearly moving
through that room on his long legs in his tight pants
showing secret parts of him, the Marlboro cigarette
hanging from his tipped lips, grinning, almost dancing when he walked, swooping down on that scene
like some great wide-winged bird living near the sea,
coming suddenly out of the blue summer sky all pink
and silver, gliding.

Said, "Opal, you've got real pretty eyes, and
someday—"

"Opal?"

"OPAL!"

"Huh?"

"Grayson says Bobby John's out back," said Diane-
Young. "Remember. 10-3."

Jesse said, "I'll walk you out."

"Real nice seeing you again, Opal," Verna Cloward
said.

"Night, Opal," said V. Chicken, and they all said
good night and good-bye, giving me big smiles.

Jesse and I walked down the long marble hall.
"You don't have to walk me out," I said.

"I want to, Opal. You didn't get a chance to say
much."

"I had the chance."

"I get that way, too."

"Why?"

"Why? Why do you?"

Shrugged my shoulders again, thought of how there
seemed no end to that long hall, like there seemed no
beginning to my conversations with Jesse Pegler. I
hoped the tuna-fish smell from inside the Baggie in
my purse wasn't leaking out, hoped he hadn't seen
the hole in my sweater.

Then I saw Bobby John standing by the butler at

the door, his best Hawaiian shirt hanging outside his fresh-ironed khaki pants, hair slicked back, cracking his knuckles, looking all around, smiling his sweet, sad smile at me. I was glad Jesse Pegler didn't have to walk out with me to the van, if that's what Bobby John'd come over in. I'd hate Jesse seeing me get into that thing.

Last thing Jesse said, "I'm going to call you, Opal."

Driving away in Bobby John's car, I gave a giggle because he said that.

"How come you're in such a good mood?" Bobby John asked me.

I should have just said back to Jesse why, what for?

"Well, I was the belle of the ball, Bobby John," I said, sounding sour as month-old milk, moods swinging back and forth, back and forth, like the clapper in a church bell. "Had myself this real rootin'-tootin' time."

"Don't expect nothing from them people and you'll never be disappointed," Bobby John said. "Did you get to talk to D. Y.?"

"She said they were watching her like a hawk because they think you're too much of an influence on her. She said to tell you 10-3."

"That's all she said?"

"That's all she said. What's 10-3 mean, anyway?"

"That's CB talk, means 'stop transmitting.' Is that all she said?"

"She said she might be going on an ACE Winning Rally, to witness," I said, "and the cook there said she'd walked all right before the healing."

"Who'd she say that to?"

"Ripper Blades' mother. . . . Bobby John, what'd you think of him?"

"What'd I think of who?"

"Bud's brother. Calls me Oh-pull. Says he's going to call me. I don't have a clue why. What for, I had a mind to ask."

"Well, if he's going to ask you out, Daddy's not going to like it."

"He's not going to ask me out."

"He might."

"He's not going to. But he's saved, anyways."

"Who says he's saved?"

"He's Guy Pegler's son, anyways."

"That's the one thing Daddy won't like," said Bobby John. "Daddy's saying Guy Pegler stole our miracle."

"I guess he sort of did, didn't he?"

We just rode along for a while with the big moon beaming down, abundance of peace, said in Psalms, so long as the moon endureth. Asked myself if Jesus was to say you can live on Ocean Road and be Jesse Pegler's girl, get notes from him, be his sweet baby, or you can be part of The Rapture—

Then Bobby John said, "She's been walking on that leg okay for a long time."

I looked up at him.

"It wore her out faking, pain was gone a long time ago. She was afraid not to fake, afraid they'd say nothing ever was wrong with her to begin with. . . . Well, we needed a miracle at The Hand."

"Whew, Bobby John. What are you telling me?"

"Nothing you're ever going to say aloud to anyone. Promise?"

"I promise."

"K. Christian Keck come all the way from Philadelphia. How you going to get a man like that to come again if nothing happens—think he'd want to come back again with nothing going on but Mrs. Bunch falling again? Opal, people don't pay when nothing happens but her going down. Daddy was worrying away, too."

"Nothing new," I said.

"Well, it don't bother you. You don't bear the brunt of it. You heard him tonight, telling me I was dumb again, telling me no one's going to leave their living room while the TV preachers got choirs of fifty and more in living color. You know how long I been hearing that?"

"Yeah, I know."

"I got Daddy on the one hand needing the bills to get paid, and I got D. Y. on the other telling me there weren't no way she could just say she could walk all right suddenly. Doctors said all along there wasn't anything wrong with her when there was. If she was to just walk all right suddenly, everybody'd say the doctors was right and she'd been faking. . . . Well, that's where the miracle come from, Opal. Right from Satan. Now we're going to pay the price."

We rode along while not talking, until Bobby John turned on his CB radio and started in on his spiel to make himself feel better.

"Put your ears on, good buddy. You don't need a 10-84 to call Him. He's God's Son and He loves you no matter what your handle is or what channel you're on. He won't break in. He only comes by invitation."

A week later, Daddy was shouting it out. "They stole our miracle, right out from under our noses!" He was so loud, folks over to the dump scavenging could likely hear him yelling from The Hand.

I was doing a count that Sunday morning, not fifty people there, unless you counted the six in the choir. Daddy made fifty-one in the whole place, and the weather was good, too. Sun was out, temperature was in the seventies.

"When the haves come down here to the have-nots for their miracles, they leave their checkbooks home! They wait until they're back up there in front of the cameras to give witness, and they wait until they're back up there with the rest of the haves to whip out their checkbooks!"

"Amen!" from Mrs. Bunch. Then everybody, "Amen!"

"Well, when The Rapture comes, and it's close at hand, I feel it in my bones, when The Rapture comes, we'll have something to say to the haves. Praise the Lord will we have something to say to them!"

Everybody: "Praise the Lord!"

"We're going to fix our eyes on their eyes and we're going to say, 'Where were you when we were needing? We were there when you were needing, but where were you when we were needing?' "

"WHERE WERE YOU?" Mrs. Bunch called out.

"The Rapture's coming!" someone else cried.

"You know it, brother!" Daddy shouted back. He came from around the lectern with his hands balled to fists, thick eyebrows scowling, voice cracking out over us like a whip: "WHEREWEREYOU? WHERE-WEREYOU? WHEREWEREYOU?"

"Where were you?"—Mrs. Bunch.

"Shout it out!" Daddy ordered.

"WHEREWEREYOU?"

Then Daddy started them chanting: "Rather be a have-not when The Rapture comes, wouldn't be a have if I could, and uh rather be a have-not when The Rapture comes, wouldn't be a have if I could, and uh," working it up like a train chugging, "rather . . . be . . . a . . . have . . . not . . . rather be . . . a . . . have . . . not . . . uh . . . rather be a . . . have-not . . . uh . . . rather be a have-not . . . uh . . . rather be a have-not, a have-not, a have-not, a have-not, a have-not—"

The real truth was deep inside me I would rather be a have, which was why The Rapture sometimes scared the living daylights out of me. When God came down to take us back up with Him, be caught in my true thoughts like a cat with my paw in the fishbowl.

After church, while Mum made dinner, I drove far down into The Hollow with Daddy, to call on Willard Peyton who was too old and frail to leave his house.

On the way there, Daddy stopped the van long enough for me to pick wild flowers from a field, to take to Mr. Peyton.

I arranged the flowers in an old Tropicana orange-juice quart, while Daddy sat on Willard Petyon's bed, in the center of his shack on Sunny Sky Drive, and held his hand.

The biggest thing in the shack besides the bed was an RCA color TV with a nineteen-inch screen, set on the floor. Mr. Petyon had it tuned in to Guy Pegler.

Daddy motioned to me to turn the sound down and said, "We missed you this morning, Willard."

"Royal, I'm heading for the barn."

"I came to pray with you, Willard."

"I sent something in to Oral Roberts, sent something to Rex Humbard, even sent something to him"—pointing at the TV—"but all their prayers don't seem to be doing any good. Worrying about my dog, Royal, who'll take him."

"These prayers are on the house, Willard," said Daddy.

While Daddy prayed for him, I looked out the window at old Yellow, Willard's dog, moping in the yard under a car up on blocks, like he had what Willard had.

Some folks from The Hand said Willard Peyton was a miser, and had more money than any one of them made in a year, stuffed in a tin can and put in the ground behind his shack.

I went out in the sun awhile, petted Yellow, waiting for Daddy to finish up. When I went back inside, the free 800 number was flashing across the bottom of the screen, for all the viewers who wanted to order the P.S. charm by phone.

"I just wonder who'll take old Yellow in," Willard Peyton said, letting his head fall back on the pillow after Daddy's prayers. "I tell you, Royal, if this is a minor stroke like they say, I'd like to know what a major one is. Old Yellow don't have no one but me."

Daddy said, "Job said in III: 25, 'That which I have greatly feared has come upon me.' When doesn't it? When doesn't it?"

Then Daddy kissed him and motioned for me to put the sound back on the TV, and we headed home.

"We could take Yellow," I said as we rode along.

"We add dog food bills to cat food bills, we'll be eating Alpo our own selves. Someone from The Hand will take the dog when the time comes."

"He doesn't have any family, does he?"

"He's the last."

"Will The Hand get the money he's rumored to have?"

"I don't know, honey," said Daddy, "but we'd lose more than we'd get, if we was to inherit it. Willard Peyton's been coming to The Hand since back in the days when we had cotton-stocking, gingham-dress, sawdust-trial revivals. He's old stock, and we'd gain nothing with his passing."

"Still and all, I wonder what he's got."

" 'The love of money is the root of all evil,' Opal. I Timothy VI: 10."

"I don't love it. I don't have it to love. I just wonder what it'd be like to have any."

"Never mind," Daddy said, sighing.

"We never seem to have any we get."

"Well, sweetheart, money's like manure, does no good till it's spread."

Another sigh from him. I got mad at myself for mentioning money, rattled on about how glad I was to be starting my new job down to Bunch Cleaners. He said he was glad I was glad, but I don't think either of us was that glad I was getting paid three and a half an hour to go through dirty clothes looking for loose change, and put clean clothes on hangers under plastic.

When we got back home, the whole house smelled of roast chicken, and Mum came out barefoot to meet us, saying, "Jesse Pegler was by to bring regards from ACE. I said what you doing here when your Daddy's live on TV now? He said it wasn't live no more. Did you know it wasn't live no more, Royal?"

"No, Arnelle, I did not. It's not my business to keep track of Guy Pegler. . . . Poor old Willard is going to croak." Daddy went over and plopped down in his Barcalounger in the living room.

Mum said to me, "Jesse Pegler said to say he was by. Calls you Oh-Pull."

I laughed and clapped my hands together. "He always says Oh-Pull."

"Says Oh-Pull," Mum giggled.

"What's got into you two?" Daddy said. "I'm telling your mother Willard Peyton's going to pass, and you two are all worked up over some boy saying a name funny."

"He was looking for you, I think," Mum told me. "He's not just some boy, Royal. He's Guy Pegler's youngest, and a real nice boy. Real nice!"

"I don't give a hoot," Daddy said.

"There's something I want to take up with you, too," Mum said, "talking of giving a hoot. I don't give a hoot for you expecting payment of any kind for a miracle our Lord performed! Royal, I didn't like you saying in your sermon the Cheeks should have wrote us a check."

"That was not what I said, Arnelle, so you didn't listen."

"You might just as well have said it. I hate to think we got money on the brain and that's all. They offered us a CheckCheek Security System, free of charge, equal in value to one thousand dollars, and that is payment enough if you wanted to accept it."

"Did he walk way over here?" I said.

"He had his daddy's fancy car."

"I'd like to know a way to get money off the brain for sure," said Daddy. "We took in peanuts again, and every bit of it was loose change. Not a dollar bill in that plate. You'd think paper was gold."

"I know a way to get it off the brain," Mum said, undoing her apron strings, meaning she wanted us to kneel down and pray.

"Amen," Daddy said, and got up from his lounge chair. "Where's Bobby John?"

"He's over to Drive-In Burger. Jesse Pegler drove him over."

Mum got down on her knees, holding on to the Barcalounger for support.

Daddy got down, and I did.

"Oh Lord," Daddy began, "help us to see the goodness through the bad. Help us to see this fine morning, the chicken smells coming from the kitchen, Opal here had a nice young fellow, son of a preacher, come calling on her—"

"Hey, Daddy!" I complained. "Don't tell Him that. That's not for sure he came to see *me*."

Eight

JESSE PEGLER

Seal and I were working for ACE that summer.

One of the things we were supposed to do was go up to teenage drivers at the sunrise service and present them with "It's Up to You" bumper stickers.

We handed out about forty, then went back to my father's study to watch the show. Seal took notes on everything: camera angles, choir members whose faces didn't "light up" as they sang, the need for more closeups of blacks and Hispanics—you name it and Seal was scribbling it across an ACE pad with her gold ACE pencil.

She was stretched out on the rug in white shorts and a white T-shirt with "IT'S UP TO YOU!" printed across it in gold letters. She had these long legs, already tanned from tennis in early June, and sun streaks through her long yellow hair. I was watching her watch my father, waiting for the end of the service, when I could finally say, "Hey, let's drive somewhere. I have Dad's car for the morning."

"Hey, the thought of driving somewhere doesn't exactly thrill me," she answered. "I've had my own car for years."

"Oh that's right," I said. "You're The Jaded Lady who's seen and done everything. What would exactly thrill you?"

"The thought of catching Reverend Cloward's eleven-o'clock service," she said. "I told your father I'd go there with good wishes from ACE. We're supposed to build up goodwill between ACE and local churches, remember?"

"That's *is* thrilling," I said. "Be sure and catch a glimpse of Dickie while you're there."

"I'd want more than a glimpse of Dickie," she said.

Dickie was my age, and he was in my class at Seaville High. All the girls were blown away by Dickie's good looks, but there was something eerie about Dickie, too. He was like a science-fiction clone of his old man. He didn't look like he'd had another parent— just the Reverend. He stood like him, walked like him, sounded like him—he had all his gestures. Even the part in his hair was the same.

"Sometimes I think you're a P.K. groupie," I said.

"Sometimes I think you're jealous."

"Sometimes I am."

"You can always come with me, Jesse."

"The thought of going to church twice in one Sunday doesn't exactly thrill *me*," I said. "I've been going to church for seventeen years."

I drove her to her house, waited for her to change clothes, and dropped her off on Main Street, at the First Methodist Church.

Seal had said what I ought to do was call on the Ringers, take Opal for a ride, something. We owe them something, she said, I feel guilty around Arnelle. Just pretend you're a male hummingbird. She laughed. The day before, we'd watched this movie called *Sex and Courtship*, sent to ACE by Faith Films. They were trying to sell it to ACE for our teenage "Play and Pray" program. There were shots of this male hummingbird showing off his dazzling plumage, stunt flying through the air to attract a female calmly perched on a branch waiting.

Even if I could talk myself into pretending I was the male hummingbird, the idea of Opal Ringer calmly perched anywhere didn't fit. Opal was more like some little cat, forced out into the wild to make her own way too soon. She was the kind of creature you'd have thought one loud noise would send her clinging to something, mewing with fear, like the cat hanging to the side of a tree, its fur on end, while dogs barked up from the ground.

But Seal told me exactly where the Ringers lived on Hog Creek Road, and I turned the car around and headed that way.

When Mrs. Ringer told me Opal wasn't there, I wound up giving Opal's brother a ride to Drive-In Burger.

He said he needed a new car, he thought—"a new secondhand one."

He said, "Riding around in this thing, I feel like I'm getting above my raisings." He was cracking his knuckles, stretching his long legs out after moving the seat back.

"This car really belongs to ACE," I said.

"Don't everything? I hear Diane-Young Cheek does, too, now. Hear she's going out with ACE to witness."

"She'll make The Helping Hand Tabernacle famous," I said.

"That'd be another miracle, wouldn't it?"

"Don't you think she'll do you some good?"

"I think she'll do you all some good," he said. "I think her folks want her out of Seaville is what I think. . . . Was that your first healing?"

"I've been to a lot of healings, Bobby John. My own grandfather could heal, or at least he could use the power of suggestion to good advantage."

"Do you think that's what happened with Diane-Young? The power of suggestion?"

"I think that had something to do with it."

"Don't that bother you any?"

"Why should it?"

"You got to ask yourself who did the suggesting."

"It doesn't matter, does it? She's off the crutch."

He asked me a lot of questions about ACE Winning Rallies, how long the tour took, who went on it, what happened, and I finally told him we weren't even sure we could raise the money for the summer one. I told him we had all we could do to stay on TV.

"We got all we can do to keep our doors open," he said. I pulled into Drive-In Burger and offered to buy him a burger, "for helping us find Diane-Young. Come on," I said. "My treat."

"I didn't come here to eat," he said. "I'm on the afternoon shift."

Then he said, "Opal'll be real pleased you came by to see her, and much obliged for the lift."

He gave me a little two-fingered salute and slammed the car door shut.

I was in charge of ACE's "Personal Touch," which my father described as "a one-man outreach operation." I was supposed to drive around to the jails and hospitals, shake hands with people, pass out our leaflets and charms, and remind everyone that *It's Up to You* was on TV every Sunday at noon.

Seal was helping my mother run the ACE cassette course, and the ACORN program (A Counselor of Reborn Neighbors).

It was Donald Divine's idea that my mother should make white her trademark. She bought an all-white wardrobe. She used our sunroom for her office, and Donald got a decorator in who filled the place with white wicker furniture, white cushions, white rugs over white ceramic tile floors, and white flowering plants.

We were a far cry from the days down South when we piled into motel rooms at day's end, and only unpacked what we needed for the next day.

Donald had even gone out and bought a white angora cat for my mother, which he named Blanche. Blanche slept over on the windowsill of the sunroom, in a white straw basket, atop a white pillow.

There were photographs taken showing my mother working there, for the front cover of the ACORN bulletin.

I stopped by the sunroom my first Monday morning on the job, the end of that June.

"Jesse," my mother said when I walked through the door, "change into a suit. Put on a tie. Sick people, people in trouble, don't want some kid in blue jeans calling on them."

"Dad didn't say anything at breakfast," I said. "Hi, Seal."

Seal was sitting there taking dictation from my mother. She said hi back and I noticed she was dressed in white, too—white dress, white sandals, even a white watchstrap.

"Your father didn't realize you were going out in the same clothes you came down to breakfast in, Jesse. Now change into a suit and tie, then come back down here, because we've got some good news."

"Super news," Seal said.

"What's so super about it?" I said, and suddenly got this shaky feeling inside it was news from Bud.

"I said change your clothes, darling, and let me finish up here with Seal. Then we'll tell you."

I went back up to my room and changed into a suit. I hated neckties, and spending my clothes allowance on them, so the few I had were real cheapos. Bud's closet was jammed with sports coats, slacks, sweaters, shirts, and ties—he'd packed only one suitcase when he took off. But we were leaving everything just as Bud had left it, orders from the old man. "You may borrow anything from me, but leave Bud's things alone."

I got a tie from the back of my father's closet, mulling over how I'd feel if they said Bud was on his way home.

At dinner last night we'd gotten another "ding."

The ding was something my father'd worked out years ago when he was out on the road. He'd dial our number, and hang up before the first ring was over. There was just a little ding sound, "A ding," my father said, "to remind you all I'm thinking of you, and I love you."

Bud always dinged us at dinnertime. It couldn't be anyone else.

He'd written my father and mother one letter after he first left, which I'd never seen, and all the other communications were dings.

"They're coming closer and closer together," my father said. "I hope that means it's getting closer to the time he'll be back with us."

"I think he's ready," my mother said. "I just feel it."

We'd interrupted our roast-beef dinner while my father bowed his head and said a prayer. He was a little teary eyed; maybe that was helped along by the two martinis he'd put away before we were called to the table. I couldn't read my father very well anymore. It was getting so the only time I could was when he came across TV. He was dynamite then, I had to give him that.

I checked the tie out in the mirror and thought about how much Bud loved summers at the beach. He and Seal were both surfers. They could spend a whole day on their backs in the sand, too, soaking up the sun, getting neat tans. My skin broke out in the sun, and the only summer sport I really liked was fishing. Seal said you had to do too many cruel things to fish—put hooks through worms, tear the faces of fish; she had a whole lecture against fishing.

When I got back down to the sunroom, my mother was in the midst of dictation: "*. . . and this is why I am personally writing to encourage you to become an ACORN.*

"*Dr. Pegler and I have talked together about what an effective ACORN you'd be! We were so impressed with the beautiful summary you wrote for us, at our request, when your cassette course ended.*

"*'Rhoda,' Guy said to me, 'could we convince blank to enroll as an ACORN? Her personality has just that certain Christian charisma we need!'*

"*We will be praying that your answer will be yes, and we are enclosing the registration form for ACORN.*

"Remember, blank, Jesus wants you to win! So do we! Sincerely."

Then my mother said, "Seal, change the thirty-dollar registration fee to fifty dollars. Have five hundred copies of this letter made up in the personalized style, using that list of names from subscribers to the cassette course. Now, honey, be very sure no letters are sent to two people from the same town. Of course, when blank is a he, substitute his for her."

I said, "It must have been really boring hearing Dad say that five hundred times. Rhoda, could we convince blank to enroll as—"

My mother cut me off. "Oh, that's just a figure of speech and you know it. That just makes being an ACORN sound more inviting."

"It sounds like a con game to me," I said.

"And you sound like Bud to me. Doesn't he sound like Bud, Seal?"

"He will when his voice gets deeper."

My mother went across the room, grabbed Blanche and Blanche's white comb, and started grooming her.

"What's the good news?" I said. "Did we hear from Bud?"

"Jesse Pegler," said Seal, "do you think if we'd heard from Bud I'd be able to sit still?"

"Seal von Hennig," I said, "do you think you'll ever give up on Bud?"

"Now, Jesse, don't be sassy," said my mother. "We just had that ding, that's all we've ever had, but that ding says he loves us."

"I never even got a ding," Seal said.

"Maybe never getting a ding says something else," I said.

"Oh, Seal, sweetheart, dinging is our family tradition," my mother said, "and I doubt Bud even knows you know what a ding would mean."

"Then what's the good news?" I said.

"Even if I never got a ding," Seal said, "I wouldn't mind seeing him coming through that door, even if he doesn't want me."

"Bud doesn't know what he wants," my mother said. "Oh, he'll be here one of these days. He'll plan it real dramatic, because Bud's vain like Blanche here. Knows she's going to be the prettiest cat in Suffolk County when I get through combing her. When the Lord blesses you with good looks, there's nothing wrong in celebrating such a blessing. Within limits, of course. Bud went overboard in the clothes department, but at least he knew not to wear jeans and sneakers to visit sick people in the hospital."

She glanced over at me, still a little mad because I'd made fun of her ACORN letter.

She said, "You look a whole lot better now, Jesse. But your father has to take you shopping. You need some new clothes. That suit's so old it'll walk by itself someday."

"Mom, I'm seventeen."

"That old!" Seal said, hitting her forehead with her palm. "Whew!"

"Nobody has to take me shopping," I went on anyway.

My mother said, "Somebody is going to be eighteen soon, which is the news we have. Tell him, Seal."

"We've got an invitation to a party, Jesse." She passed a card across to me.

You are Invited to Dinner Before The Last Dance on the occasion of Diane-Young Cheek's
18th birthday
July 26
7 P.M.

Wear a hat representing your astrology sign, in keeping with The Zodiac theme of the dance. Transportation to the dance will be provided. A table is reserved for Diane-Young's guests. Bring a date.

Bud always said if he was my sign, he'd lie about it. Virgo, according to Bud, was the dullest sign of the zodiac. Virgos are drawer straighteners, Bud always said. Gemini, according to Bud, was the best sign. No need to ask what sign Bud was.

"Is this the big news?" I said. "I do the jails on Saturday nights."

"Oh, everybody's going to The Last Dance," my mother said. "The jails can wait."

Seal said, "I'm on the hot line Saturday nights, but I won't be July twenty-sixth. Tell him the rest, Mrs. Pegler."

"You tell him, honey. If it wasn't for you we wouldn't have known Diane-Young Cheek from boo. We'd never have gone there for dinner or any of it."

"That was the thrill of all time, too," I said. "Dinner there."

"You just watch that mouth of yours, Jesse," my mother snapped.

Coming home from the Cheeks' that night she'd said Whew! I'm just glad that's behind us. If I never hear another word about Rudolph Nureyev, or Margot Fonteyn, or Vera Volkova, it'll be too soon, and she never even inquired anything to do with me, if I had a hobby—anything. My father said Ye have heard of the patience of Job. Job's Job, my mother said, I was a guest in their home and never once got asked a question about myself.

"The good news," said Seal, "is there was something enclosed with this invitation. A check made out to ACE."

"Hallelujah," I said.

"Hallelujah is right!" my mother said. "The check is for ten thousand dollars."

I let out a slow whistle.

"It's to get our Winning Rally on the road," Seal said.

My mother said, "Thank you, Lord."

"Jesse?" Seal said. "Arnelle told me once the one thing in the world Opal wished she could do would be go to The Last Dance. Now we owe them that much. We'll make up a table. You and Opal, me and Dickie, Verna and—"

"Wait a minute," I said. "You and Dickie?"

"We don't want Reverend Cloward's nose out of joint," said my mother. "He's out ten thousand dollars, after all."

After I left my mother and Seal, I walked down to my father's study to get his car keys.

Donald Divine was with him. My father was staring out the window, complaining that he hated to ask Igor Sonnebend for any more favors.

Donald was pouring himself more coffee. "It's a favor to Igor, too, Guy," Donald said. "Igor's going to trade that jet in on a new one. If we can persuade him to donate it to ACE, he'll have a tax deduction and we'll have a plane that will carry our whole crew on crusades."

My father turned around, saw me, and said, "Jesse, that tie isn't right for you, son."

"Hi, Jesse," Donald said. "When you leave, I'd like a ride to the train station."

"It's your tie," I said.

"It's right for me but not for you, son," said my father. "I love you, but not in a Countess Mara tie. Can't you pick out one that's not so fancy?"

"Why wear one at all?" Donald said. "Aren't you going to Riverhead jail today?"

"He's going to Oceanside Hospital," my father said. "He has to wear a tie. Put on one of my ACE ties, son."

"Maybe you should lay out my clothes for me the night before," I said.

My father laughed his nervous laugh and said, "Nobody's picking on you, Jesse. I remember one time Bud showed up for a service in a pair of Nikes. He was doing a solo, Donald, and I made him put on my shoes, which were a size too small for him. Well"— my father began breaking up over his own story— "well, these shoes were pinching him. And the song he was singing was 'I Can't Even Walk.' You know. It goes 'I can't even walk without holding Your hand.'

Well, every time Bud paused between walk and without, I thought I'd double over with laughter, knowing what I knew about those shoes being too small for him." He took his glasses off and wiped away tears. "Oh, my, that was some morning!"

Then he reached in his pants pocket and took out keys and three ten-dollar bills, handing them to me. "The money's not for you, Jesse. Now that you're on the payroll, you'll get your check bimonthly like the rest of us. The money is your Godspeed allowance."

"I don't know what you mean by a Godspeed allowance."

"I mean that if you meet someone in the hospital who's complaining about the food, step out and buy him a sandwich, and wish him Godspeed. Maybe someone you'll meet is worried about a friend's birthday coming up, and you'll want to wish her Godspeed by buying her a birthday card for her friend, putting a stamp on it, addressing the envelope for her. Do you see what I mean, Jesse? Don't just deliver your spiel, hand out our charm, and go on your way. Try to be of real help."

"We ought to take our camera in with him someday," said Donald, "and get some film of it. That's bottom-line Christianity."

"I like that!" my father said. "Bottom-line Christianity . . . Well, so many times we aren't of any practical assistance. Bud taught me that. Bud said, Dad, don't just give them prayers. Give them something up front: money for a pack of cigarettes, a dime to make a phone call. People remember that more than they remember prayers. Bud's right."

"Particularly now that he's gone," said Donald.

"Gone but not forgotten," I said.

"Oh, not forgotten!" said Donald.

"Are you two ganging up on me?" my father said.

He came over and put his arm around me. "I love you, Jesse. Good luck today."

"Thanks, Dad. I love you, too, sir."

"Change the tie."

* * *

On my way to the train station with Donald, he said, "You know, your dad is convinced Bud's coming home soon. He's going to pitch a sermon to him, and we're going to have a charm made up based on it. . . . Do *you* really think Bud watches him Sunday mornings, Jesse?"

"How do I know what Bud does anymore?" I said.

"Exactly," Donald said. "Exactly. But your dad's set on pitching a sermon to him. The Happiest Man thing, remember it?"

"Yeah, I remember it."

"What's funny?"

"Nothing," I said. "Everything."

I could remember my dad years ago, under the tent, coat off, tie loosened, shirt sleeves rolled up. First he'd play the part of the king. "Go forth and bring me the shirt of the happiest man in my kingdom!"

It was an old favorite of Dad's—a story about a king whose oracle told him the only way he could be happy was to wear the shirt of the happiest man in his kingdom. My father stretched the story out with all sorts of sidelines, until the ending when the oracle, crouched in this fawning attitude, announces with this little whiny voice, "My king and master, we have finally located the happiest man in your kingdom."

Then Dad straightened up, brought his fist forward, and slapped it into his palm, shouting, "Bring me his shirt!"

The oracle, wringing his hands, mincing around, finally whimpering, "My king and master, the happiest man in your kingdom has no shirt."

When we were little, Bud and I loved that story. So did everyone under the tent, in the old days.

Donald said, "We're going to have a charm made of a little bare-chested man." He heaved a sigh.

I didn't say anything, just took the left turn toward the train station. My secret self was laughing it up in my head.

"If you ask me, it's a foolish idea," Donald said.

"He hasn't told that one in a long time," I said.

"Right now isn't the time to take it out of moth-balls, either," Donald said. "We're telling people you can do *anything*—it's up to you! We're not saying be glad you don't have a pot to pee in!"

"No, we're certainly not saying that," I said, pulling up next to a taxi stand.

"A humble backwoods ministry is one thing," Donald said. "A television ministry is another."

"I think the television ministry is what got to Bud," I said. "I think all the fund raising—"

Donald didn't let me finish. "Without all the fund raising, your dad would still be wasting his God-given talents talking to two hundred ne'er-do-well bump-kins who couldn't collectively drop three hundred dollars into a cardboard box! What the hell did Bud ever know about business? He likes to go skinny-dipping over to his girl friend's fifty-foot swimming pool, but he doesn't like to think how her old man got so he could afford that pool!" The train whistle blasted and Donald waited, then in a softer voice said, "What about God saying to Solomon, I will give thee riches, and wealth? He gave Job twice as much as Job ever had before all his afflictions!"

One thing about Donald: You could always count on the fact he did his research.

He was reaching behind the front seat of our Se-ville for his Gucci briefcase with the gold ACE insignia embossed across the leather.

"What about Abraham, Isaac, Jacob, David, and Joseph of Arimathea?" said Donald.

"I'm not as well informed as you are, Donald."

"Well get informed, Jesse. It wouldn't hurt any. A television ministry is a family business, boy."

"Your train's pulling in," I said.

"I see it," he said, and then he finished his point. "God made them all rich, as a reward! That was God's will, that they become rich men! So what is all this no-shirt bullshit!"

*   *   *

Sometimes I forgot what a real celebrity my father was, and how many watched *It's Up to You*. There were security guards at the end of our driveway, and an elaborate CheckCheek Security system built into our house, but day to day Dr. Guy Pegler was just my old man. . . . ACE's central offices were in Riverhead, and a staff in Massachusetts handled all our mail, and sent out all our merchandise. . . . Our small Seaville staff handled the hot line, the outreach program, and public relations, from the office in The Summer House.

My father liked to say he kept a low profile in Seaville, and we rarely went to public places there. About the only place he went when he did manage to get some free time was The Hadefield Club. No one there made a fuss over him. The place was filled with celebrities. . . . At Seaville High, I was just another kid.

But the moment I arrived at Oceanside Hospital, I was reminded that I wasn't just another kid, I was his kid, and sick people came down the halls in their bathrobes and slippers to get a look at me. Some of them even wanted *my* autograph, and said they remembered seeing me on TV.

I even found myself sounding like my father, although I guess I didn't have his spiel down as pat as I thought I did.

Because when I said, "We just want you to know we want you to win. So does Jesus," one old man in a ward bed began waving his hands, as if he was waving flies off his face, saying, "No, no, no, no.

"You got it backward, boy," he said. "Jesus wants me to win, and so do you. That's how your father says it." He looked like he was using his dying strength to tell me off. His face turned red, and he'd raised himself up on his elbows to get a good look at me.

"How do you do, sir. I'm Jesse Pegler."

"I know who you are," he said. "Want a dog?"

"I beg your pardon?"

"I asked you if you wanted a dog!"

I was taking out one of our gold-plated charms when he said, "You can keep that gold thingamajig. If you want to give me something, give me peace of mind."

He couldn't hold himself up any longer, so he sank back into the pillows while I moved closer to him. "I'm worrying about my dog," he said. "I'm heading for the barn, boy. I got carted over here early this morning and they put my dog in the animal shelter."

I remembered what my father said when he gave me the Godspeed money, and I reached in my pocket for my ACE notebook. "What's your name, sir?"

"Willard Peyton. My dog's named Yellow."

I started taking down the information, telling him not to worry.

"He's an old dog," he said. "It'll be hard to find him a home."

"We'll find him one."

He told me he went to church at The Helping Hand Tabernacle, but since he'd been sick he'd been watching *It's Up to You*.

Behind me, people were starting to line up for charms.

"Yellow's fourteen years old," he said. "I don't know who'll want a dog that old."

"Mr. Peyton," I said, "I'll see that Yellow has a good home, if I have to take him myself."

"You promise me, boy?"

"I promise you," I said, and I didn't have any doubt I could keep the promise, knowing Seal's soft side when it came to animals.

I left the old man with a smile on his face.

It'd been a long time since I'd felt that good about anything I'd done in the name of ACE.

On my way back into Seaville, I stopped at the animal shelter, which was closed for the day. I left a note saying I'd pick up the dog the next morning.

Then I went to a pay phone and called the Challenge hot line, knowing Seal was on duty. I asked her if she wanted to go to Sweet Mouth.

"Your father's just had a crank call," she said. ("Crank call" was ACE's euphemism for anything from a stream of obscenities to a death threat. We got a lot of crank calls.) "I've also got a battered woman calling back in half an hour. Your mother's calling around to find a family to take her in for the night. Are you finished at the hospital?"

I told her she had a new dog named Yellow, filling her in on all the details while I fed another quarter to the coin box.

"You'd better let the Ringers know he's at Ocean-side Hospital," she said. "Now's your chance to invite Opal to the Cheeks' dinner, and The Last Dance."

"Seal, I don't know if that's such a good idea. I don't even know Opal."

"Get to know her," Seal said. "Ask *her* to go to Sweet Mouth with you."

"I wish you could get away," I managed to get in before she said, "Jesse, please, we're so busy here I can't stay on the line. Arnelle's been super to my family! Another call's coming in now, Jesse. . . . Will you do that for me?"

I didn't say anything.

"Do it for ACE," she said. "ACE owes the Ringers something."

"If I do it," I said, "I'll do it for you."

I don't think she even heard me.

Nine

OPAL RINGER

"I hope this is going to be all right with Daddy," Mum said. "What'd he say again?"

I was tearing things off hangers, trying them on, throwing them on the bed, seemed like nothing was right to wear with him.

"First he said Willard Peyton was at Oceanside, said we ought to know that."

"That's on Daddy's message sheet. They took him over early this morning."

"Then he just says would you like to go to Sweet Mouth?"

"In his car?"

"I don't know in his car."

"He come in his car last time."

Right after he called, Mum came home from the von Hennigs and found me running around my bedroom like a chicken with her head cut off, trying to get dressed. Daddy and Bobby John were down in The Hollow on a sick call. Mum had said she didn't like it that I'd said I'd go out with him when I didn't have permission. I said back who was I going to get permission *from?*

She put her coat away and brought her Good Living Comic in to look at, while she sat in my rocker. She was trying to finish the story of Daniel in the lion's den. Daddy got back issues with the covers off

from The Upper Room, and when we finished with
them we gave them out at The Hand.

"A boy that calls the same day for a date isn't
showing respect, though," Mum said. "Your daddy
called a week ahead."

"Mum, please. I've got to find something to wear!
Help me."

"Wear that nice red wool sweater Seal gave you,
honey."

"And let him know I wear her hand-me-downs?"

"It don't have her name on it."

"She could be there in The Sweet Mouth."

"The thing I think about is who's going to get the
blame if Daddy don't like it when he gets home."

"Well don't think about it, then."

"I think about it. Right here after they pulled
Daniel up from the pit with all the lions? Well, then
they put his accusers and their families in the pit and
the animals tore *them* to pieces instead. Someone
always pays."

"Mum, I'm going out on a *date*. I'm not being
lowered into a pit of lions!"

"I'm just saying I hope I'm doing the right thing
letting you go," she said. "The color's gone to your
face like you got a fever. Anything you put on's going
to be sweat in you're so excited."

"You think I want to hear I'm going to sweat in
what I got on?"

Mum shook her head and said, "Whatever's got you
worked up so you shout at your own mum that way is
Satan's doing."

"I'm sorry, Mum. Can't I be excited?"

"Excited's one thing and sassy is another thing."

"I'm just a little amazed. Calls me up and says
some dumb thing about we ought to know where
Willard Peyton is, then says want to go out to The
Sweet Mouth?"

"And you says yes without permission. That's the
killer."

"Oh, Mum, that's not a killer. I got a date. That's

not a killer." I went over and put my arms around
her from behind and she patted my hands. Then she
swallowed hard and come to the real point, I guess.

"You don't know much about boys, sweetheart.
Boys and cars."

"He's a P.K., that's what he calls himself. A preacher's kid."

"Your daddy's a preacher's kid, too. Don't mean
they're not human. Honey, boys can't help themselves,
see? Boys got a different makeup."

"I know the facts of life, Mum. I took health two
years ago."

"Well, health might not have taught you boys and
cars is a bad mix."

"We're going to The Sweet Mouth, Mum." I sat
down on my bed to get my breath.

"In a car," Mum said, and the color was to her own
face then. "Don't let nothing happen in that car, you
hear me? He stops that car, you get out, tell him you
want to take a walk. A parked car off somewheres in
the woods carries three passengers—a boy, a girl, and
Satan."

"Mum, are you going to put your shoes on before
he comes?"

"Don't change the subject, Opal Ringer. I never
met a guest at the door in my bare feet yet, and you
know it."

"I don't know it. No one ever came to the door for
me."

"I got time to put on my shoes and you got time to
hear me out."

"I'm listening," I said. I hugged my arms in my
underwear, heart pounding.

"Oh honey lamb, I want this to be a nice time. He's
a nice boy, too. It isn't that. It isn't that."

"Guy Pegler's son's gotta be saved. All Daddy said
was make sure he's saved."

"Satan tempts the saved more often than the unsaved, honey. The unsaved's already in his camp,
don't you see? He's a nice boy, couldn't wish nicer for

you if we'd ordered it from the Lord, but I'm just telling you be on your guard. Satan loves a setup, honey."

"Well I'm no setup."

"I'm talking about a boy and a car, honey. That's a setup. You just remember something my own mum told me. Promise?"

"I promise."

"You just remember no one's going to buy the cow if he can get the milk free."

Remember the first time I ever came into The Sweet Mouth Soda Shoppe with him?

It was this sweet summer night with a wind so soft and warm, felt like a kitten crawling past you an inch from your face, just barely brushing by your skin, and the moon beginning yellow in the deep-blue sky, stars starting to pop out, a plane flying through them you watched to be sure was a plane and not a falling star to wish on.

He held open the door for me and I just stood there, so you probably saw that, and he said, "Go ahead," and I did.

Every single one of you was in there, it seemed like. I know all your faces so well.

Look what the cat dragged in, I think you were saying. Get a load of who just waltzed in with who.

Not a one of your knees ever shook the way mine shook that June night, and under my arms I'd already soaked through so I kept my elbows pinned to my waist, my heart ready to tear through my skin and take off on its own if I'd let it.

He said, "All the booths are taken. Do you mind sitting at the counter?"

I do secret things to make things more, like fixing in my head the song playing when we came in, wrote it down when I got home in the back of my Bible.

Wrote: *Baby, the Rain Must Fall.*

Under it, the date, and *S. Mouth. S.Shoppe.*

That was the night no one there spoke to me. "Hi" to Jesse; to Jesse, "Hello!" "How's it going?"

But my eyes were not met.
You think I don't remember that?
I still do.

I guess that was the night he told me about getting
Yellow from the animal shelter the next day, and
giving him to V. Chicken.

Half of what he said I heard, and half I didn't, and
some of what he said I only heard the tail end of.

I was trying to pick up my glass of cherry Coke
without letting the sweat smell get out from under
my armpit. I was trying to watch the ones in the
booths when they couldn't tell I was watching them.
I could probably still sit down and write out what
every girl in that place was wearing. I was working
out ways to get the glass to my lips without the rim
hitting my teeth, beating out a tattoo. I was trying to
curl my fingers under and hide my nails so he wouldn't
see they were short, not like theirs so long and pointed, and mine had no moons, was the first time I'd
even known I didn't have them, made a vow then and
there to get them.

When the little balls of fire started up toward the
ceiling, Jesse asked me, "Did you ever do that, Opal?"

"What are they?"

Everyone was laughing and pointing at them.

Jesse passed me a little wad of tissue from a bowl
on the counter.

Across the tissue in blue writing was *Amaretti di
Saronno*.

"Inside are little almond cookies," Jesse told me.
"You take the tissue off and make it into a tower, like
this."

He finally got the tissue folded so it could stand.

"What you do is light it," he said, "and make a
wish. If it goes all the way to the ceiling, you get
your wish. Halfway, you half get it. If it fizzles out on
you and doesn't rise, you don't get your wish."

He helped me fix one with his tiny hands. We built
two, and then he struck a match.

They both went up together, all the way.

"Do you want to know my wish?" he said. "I wished you'd go to a party with me."

"Well, I will," I said, and Jesse just laughed, throwing his head back, his eyes shut, face lit up like someone slain in the spirit. "Don't you even want to know where it is, who's giving it?"

I shrugged, and he reached out and hugged me once with his arm. "Oh, Opal . . . What'd you wish?"

"I wished we could get out of here," I said.

"We can!" he laughed. "Come on."

When I tell you what I really wished, you won't laugh.

But right then and there you would have.

"Opal Ringer," Mum said to me once, "you think about them too much. You think they think about you? You think about them, but they don't think about you, so now you're lopsided, honey. You got to straighten yourself out."

"I know it," I said.

I knew it.

He carried both our shoes under his arm, after we tried walking on the too-soft sand in them. His tie was hanging down and flying in the wind, sweet face, and I would have said I don't think we should while we were already going ahead because we couldn't stop ourselves.

His coat was around my shoulders and I was holding the empty sleeves thinking of them filled with his flesh and bones, hanging on to me like I hung on to them.

He said, "What sign are you, Opal?"

"You mean astrology?"

"Yes. I'm a drawer straightener. That's what Bud calls Virgos."

"Bud calls them that?" I said. "What does that mean?"

"That we're fussy or something. You know Bud. He's always got some smart remark."

"One day he told me I had real pretty eyes," I said. "He said, Opal, you've got real pretty eyes. . . ." *And someday . . .*

Jesse just shrugged.

I said, "I wonder when he'll be back. Will he come back this summer?"

"Who knows?" Jesse said.

I felt happy thinking about Bud, walking with Jesse on the sand by the ocean, those two the only boys I ever cared anything about, mixing them up in my mind sometimes, like they were one person. Even though it wasn't true I sometimes felt I knew Bud better, knew Bud's heart, from knowing how he was with V. Chicken.

Jesse asked me again what sign I was.

"I'm Pisces, born February 28th," I said, "but Daddy says astrology is from the anti-Christ. Says we shouldn't look up our forecasts in the newspaper because it's Satan's talk."

"Do you believe that?"

"I believe in The Rapture," I said.

"Do you really, Opal?"

"Sure, don't you?"

"I haven't figured out what I believe in."

"We shall all be changed, the Bible says. I believe that."

Jesse made his voice real deep and mysterious sounding, quoting from the Bible, " 'Behold, I shew you a mystery; We shall not all sleep, but we shall all be changed.' "

"That's right!" I said. "When we meet Jesus in the sky! I believe in that."

"I wish I could."

"You can. You just believe. Mum says you go to heaven without even dying when The Rapture comes."

"How does your mum feel about astrology?"

"Same way he does. It's from the anti-Christ."

"That party I just mentioned? It's a dinner party at the Cheeks'. You have to wear a hat that represents your zodiac sign."

"How come?"

"The theme of the dance this year is The Zodiac. The dinner's before the dance. Have you ever been to the dance? I haven't."

"What dance you talking about?"

"Have you heard of The Last Dance? I'm inviting you if you want to go, Opal. Do you dance? Do you want to go?"

"Do I want to go? I wanted to go to that thing my whole life!"

"Now you're going."

"Now I'm going!"

We ran like fools, I swear my feet ran on the air with the earth down below me, and by the time we stopped, we were past the dunes and up to where the car was parked. I panted like an old dying dog, caught my breath, and felt my heart hammer; well, go ahead, hammer now, you got a good reason for once, told myself.

He leaned against the car, out of breath too.

"I'll brush your feet off," I said and he caught me before I could bend over to do it.

"You do yours. I'll do mine. It's almost nine o'clock."

("Have her back by nine," Mum said when we left the house. I said, "Moo," and she gave me a look.)

When we got inside the car our breaths came back finally, and I felt so lonely and happy, let my hand next to him stay free on the seat beside us, wondering when he'd take it.

I said, "What did you really think of me the first time you ever saw me?" I even shut my eyes. *Darling . . . Someday . . .* I waited, hear a pin drop.

Next thing I knew the car motor was going, he was looking over his shoulder and backing out. "I thought you looked embarrassed because we'd come to the healing."

"Embarrassed? Is that your name for it?"

You never know what you're going to say or do. You never see behind things. You never know what you really wanted when things were going on, later told yourself well, what I wanted was for him to kiss me, for him to be Bud, say my name a hundred times, lips on the flesh of my cheeks, but that doesn't mean you really did right then and there. That's what amazes me.

After that, Jesse Pegler called me a few times at the house. He wanted to know if Mum said I could go to the party and the dance. He wanted to help me figure out what hat I could fix up to wear.

I think Daddy's nose was out of joint from the time I went out with Jesse without asking his permission. I know Daddy didn't like me going to the party and the dance, either, said he wouldn't say yes and he wouldn't say no. Said I should ask Jesus to tell me what to do.

"Royal, one time won't hurt her," Mum said.

" 'One time won't hurt' is Satan's own slogan," said Daddy. "But make your plans, make your plans if you can square it with your own conscience, Opal. Just don't tie up the phone talking to that boy about it. Folks from The Hand have to reach us."

But he also added, "Seems like your fingers are around that mouthpiece or dunked in the water bowl, one or the other."

It wasn't water in the bowl anyway, but honey and vinegar I was using to force back my cuticles and bring up my moons. I'd read up on what to do back where the beauty books were in the Seaville Library.

Then one Saturday night Brother Barker Dudley came to our house from over in Riverhead, to talk about growing legs with Daddy. He was this roly-poly man, unordained, in a black suit with a diamond ring in his little finger, no hair, and sweat always on his upper lip. He smelled sweet from something he put on his face, and stood as near as he could to the floor fan. It was a scorcher night and Mum had her shoes on unlaced, sat in the armchair trying to make a breeze with *Woman's Day*.

Bobby John's back had been giving him trouble. I

think the load on his heart over faking the healing was reaching around to his back. He wasn't talking much to me, but he was always mumbling, "Recover themselves out of the snare of the devil, who are taken captive by him." I'd ask him what good it did to keep repeating it, and he'd say he didn't even know he was saying it under his breath. He was telling Brother Dudley about the pain under his left shoulder and his stiff neck, and Daddy was saying so much of it was in his head it wasn't worth talking about to Brother Dudley. "Your problems is mental," Daddy told him.

That was all going on in our front room when the phone rang. I got off the couch fast and Daddy gave me the eye. "Not now, if it's him again, Opal."

"I know it," I said.

It was him, asking me if I wanted to go down for a soda or a cherry Coke.

"I can't because we got company."

"I hope you're thinking about your hat. Pisces is two fish swimming in opposite directions. Your lucky day is Friday."

"Yesterday was Friday and it wasn't so lucky," I said. "Five minutes to five, old Mrs. Farraday brung in every wool thing they had in their house for cleaning and storage."

I smiled to myself because it made him laugh hard, pictured him tossing his head back, a lock of his soft, yellow hair falling near his blue eyes, and him brushing it back with his small hand.

I said, "I didn't get out of that place before twenty after. Mrs. Bunch goes, 'Staple a blue slip to each item and write it up on the pink slip.' I go, 'It's five to five,' and she goes, 'I can tell time, Opal, well as you can.' "

Daddy shouted in, "OPAL!"

"I'll be on Dad's show next Sunday," Jesse said. "I just wanted to tell you to watch it. Sounds like someone wants you. I'll say good-bye."

"Good-bye."

"Good-bye."

He laughed. "Well, hang up, Opal."

"Good-bye," I said, and put down the phone's arm.

My face felt warm, and when I got back into the front room, Daddy was watching me real closely, frowning.

"Did it ever occur to you that your trouble might be you've got one leg a little shorter than the other?" Brother Dudley asked Bobby John.

"We didn't make you come all the way here to check out my son, Brother Dudley," said Daddy. "There's nothing wrong with his *legs*."

"Well, let's check it out, anyway," Brother Dudley said.

Bobby John sat down in a chair Mum brought in from the kitchen and took off his shoes, stuck his legs out.

Brother Dudley knelt down to inspect them.

"Whew!" Mum said, waving *Woman's Day*. "Your socks are high, Bobby John!"

"I didn't know I was going to take my shoes off," said Bobby John.

"That aroma doesn't bother me one bit," Brother Dudley said. "If it did, the Lord wouldn't be growing legs through me."

Brother Dudley drew a finger across the sweat beads on his upper lip, shook it, then took hold of Bobby John's feet. "Ah ha!" he said. "See here?"

"What do you see?" said Bobby John.

Mum had put down the magazine and was opening a box of Good & Plenty.

"Anyone wants one, I'll pass it," Mum said, shaking the box.

"Bobby John," said Brother Dudley, "your right leg is about three quarters of an inch shorter than your left one."

"Is it?" Bobby John said.

"That might explain all the back trouble, stiff neck, and I bet sometimes you even have trouble straightening up."

"I swear I do," said Bobby John.

Then Brother Dudley began praying, right there down on one knee, holding Bobby John's right foot. "I feel God wants me to pray for this leg, praise God. Lengthen this leg, straighten out this misalignment with Your power. I'm praying in the spirit that the power will come through me to level this leg. Heal!"

"Praise the Lord," Daddy joined in.

"I can feel You use me, Jesus! I can feel this man's foot growing."

"Praise the Lord, I can feel that," said Bobby John.

Mum was leaning forward, holding her face with her hands. She started in softly, "In the name of Jesus, shum ba la, shum ba la—"

"It's doing it, it's doing it, it's doing it," Brother Dudley was chanting.

"Praise the Lord,"—Daddy.

I said, "Praise the Lord."

". . . doing it, doing it, *done!*" Brother Dudley said.

Brother Dudley got to his feet. "I think you're going to feel a lot better, Bobby John, if not all better."

Bobby John said, "I do feel a little better." He was looking at his legs stretched out in front of him.

"Did it grow?" I asked him.

"I do think it did," said Bobby John.

He got up and walked around. "I swear it might have."

Then Brother Dudley gave a whoop and hollered, "Unspeakable joy!"

That was how leg growing came to be introduced at The Helping Hand Tabernacle.

Before Brother Dudley left, he said, "My usual cut is sixty percent of the collection plate, but because of the hard times, Royal, Arnelle, I'm going fifty-fifty with you."

"You're not lying, Bobby John?" Daddy asked him when Brother Dudley drove off.

"Daddy, I don't like being called a liar!" Bobby John's troubles were making him testy; he could flare up at anything.

"Grandfather Ringer grew legs," Mum said.

"There's no doubt legs can be grown," Daddy said. "I just don't like any faking."

I could hear all this from downstairs while I sat up in my bedroom rocker.

"Daddy, if you're calling me a fake, you're causing a breach between us nothing's going to mend," Bobby John hollered. "I might know of fakes, but I never faked myself, no matter how Satan tempted me."

"He's not calling you a fake," Mum said. "He's just checking, honey, since we don't know the man, just know he's charismatic."

"What fakes you know of, I'd like to know," said Daddy.

"Oh, we all know of fakes. He's just saying what we all know, Royal."

Warm nights made me ache with longing for nothing I knew about, and I let the light breeze brush my face, held my arms with my fingers, the Bible in my lap. I had the little lamp on, atop my card table, and a pen in my lap because I felt like writing something down.

I could hear them going at it downstairs, tuned them out, tuned them in, enjoying the smell of the fresh coffee Mum was perking, thinking what would I write? Why would I want to write anything? What was getting into me?

"Well, maybe we could try him out, don't hurt to try him out," Daddy was saying.

"Daddy," Bobby John answering him, "it's what we need. The congregation's dwindling down to nothing and we're not fighting back!"

"Don't talk to me about fighting back. Your own girl friend left us soon as she got healed, didn't even witness to us, witnessed up to them!"

"She was from them, Royal," Mum said. "She was never from us."

I opened the Bible to the flyleaf where I wr time.

Baby, the Rain Must Fall.
June 28, 7:15 P.M.
S. Mouth S. Shoppe.

The telephone rang and my heart gave a leap, but my alarm said eleven-thirty, and I doubted he'd dare call that late at night.

But I listened until I heard Daddy bellow, "Yes, this is Reverend Ringer!"

I unscrewed the top of the pen and held it ready, then it wrote itself seemed like, right under *S. Mouth S. Shoppe.*

Wrote: *Unspeakable joy!*

I let the ink dry, waited, put my finger across the words, smiling, and the little wind coming in, blowing the curtains like something little and alive moving gently behind them, nudging so sweetly at them.

When I came away from wherever it was I drifted to, I heard Daddy saying Willard Peyton was dead.

I got up and went across to the door.

"We lost him," Daddy said.

"God called him," said Mum.

Daddy said, "Seems that he left some money, poor old Willard, but I'm told he left five thousand dollars."

"Well, you can't take it with you," Mum said. "Who'd he leave it to?"

"That's the killer," Daddy said, "though the good Lord knows I wouldn't count it any kind of a blessing to profit from Willard's passing."

"We got five thousand dollars, Daddy?" Bobby John said.

Daddy said, "We don't. Guy Pegler does."

Ten

JESSE PEGLER

Donald Divine said Seal was a dynamite-looking girl and a real sweetheart for taking in Yellow, but she wasn't a Pegler, and Yellow's story had to be told about a Pegler.

"The whole point we want to get across," said Donald, "is that Guy Pegler is flesh and blood, not just an image coming on the tube Sunday mornings. He lives in a house, he's got a wife and kids, he worries about the oil bill, he's part of the family of man but he's also a *family man*."

So I found myself up on the white-and-gold balcony one Sunday morning, trying to keep my knees from knocking, and the gold tassels on my father's blue robes from blowing in my eyes, while my father did his best to make us look like "just folk."

Somehow we'd pulled Yellow up there with us before we got on camera, Donald supporting him from behind, steadying his old legs every time one slipped, and telling him, "You're a good old boy."

"What a face on this old mutt!" Donald said. "We ought to rename him Gold. I could sell Christmas trees to Scrooge with this guy for bait."

It was the Sunday of the "Happiest Man" sermon, but we cut out the lead-in hymn from The Challenge Choir, and put my father and me and Yellow in the spot.

". . . and that poor old man, dying, having already made his peace with that idea, was only worried about one thing now: his dog, a mutt he'd loved with all his heart for fourteen years, faithful companion, there every night on his hearth looking up at him, wagging his tail, how many of us haven't known the simple, lovely feeling of having our dog at our feet on an evening for comfort?"

My father paused, and then asked softly: "Could any of us die in peace knowing our old, loyal, mutt dog was in some crowded animal shelter, thrust from his familiar surroundings to a filthy, cement-floored environment where no one would even know or care about his name, there to stay *maybe* until he died of a broken heart? Looking up every time the shelter door opened, expecting to see his master, until that expectancy turned into disappointment, daily realizing on one was coming for him. And maybe worse. You know animal shelters can only shelter those poor, unwanted, unclaimed critters for so long. That's a fact of life."

On and on until finally he said, "I wonder how many people heard him say he was worried about his dog? I wonder how long that old man lay there with that burdening worry before someone—and I'm proud to say it was my own son—heard him. Jesse, would you like to introduce Yellow? And I pray with all my heart that old man has some heavenly way of looking down right now."

The cameras zoomed in on Yellow and me.

Yellow was dancing around while I held him, wagging his tail, then trying to jump up on his frail, old legs and lick my chin.

I said, "Well, Dad, he's just had a big breakfast, and he's ready for a run, and then a long nap."

"Not up on our couch in the living room, I hope." My father chuckled. "I sat down on that couch last night and there were some very suspicious yellow hairs on my dark suit when I got back up." Ha ha, from the audience.

"He's got his own bed now," I said, and I don't remember what else I managed to get out, but before I knew it the camera was back on my father and he was shouting: "Do all you can! To all you can! In all the ways you can! As often as you can! For as long as you can!"

And The Challenge Choir came in at the end, thundering out, "Brighten the Corner Where You Are."

Some ACE staff members helped me get Yellow back down the stairs and into the vestry before my old man started his sermon.

Seal was waiting for me. She threw her arms around me and said, "Oh, Jesse, that was just super! Aren't you pleased?"

"I am now."

We walked hand in hand down to my house with Yellow, people in their cars smiling and waving at us as we passed the lot.

At noon we sat together in the living room to watch the show.

Even if Yellow had wanted to, he couldn't have gotten his old bones up on the couch. He flopped down on the rug with his head on his paws, while Seal and I sank into the couch cushions and stuck our feet up on the coffee table.

We watched through to the end, my father in top form, acting out The Oracle hunting down The Happiest Man.

As soon as he'd finished, the choir began, "*Run, climb, reach for a star*," and the phone rang.

"That's Dickie," Seal said. "I'll get it."

"Dickie?" I said.

"Dickie Cloward," she said, walking over to the telephone. "I told him to call me here."

I got down on all fours and nuzzled Yellow while she talked to him. She was saying super this and super that, laughing a lot, telling him she'd designed a hat with an arrow going through it to wear to the

Cheeks' party. She was telling him to just wear horns, Taurus was the bull.

After she hung up, she came across and sat down on the floor with me.

"Dickie said to tell you he thought you were just super!"

I didn't say anything. I was ducking Yellow, who was trying to lick my face.

"Dickie's Taurus on the cusp of Gemini, so I said he should just rig up some horns on a cap, for Taurus the bull. It'd be super."

"Yeah," I said.

"He really did think you were super, Jesse. He likes you a lot."

"Okay."

"He said you were really super to Opal up at the Cheeks'."

"You ought to find another adjective besides 'super,'" I said.

She looked at me, surprised.

"What's the matter with you, anyway?" she said.

The cost of televising *It's Up to You* ate up ACE funds as fast as we could raise them. Donald and my father spent all their spare time dreaming up new gimmicks for fund raising, and Seal and I were working overtime to help get each new show off the ground.

That Sunday afternoon our project was The Good Turn Tree. There was an enormous pine tree beside The Summer House, and we were supposed to tie a ribbon to it for everyone who did a "good turn" by sending in money to keep us on the tube.

Donald had figured out that we'd been stressing family four weeks straight, and it was time to shift to country. He wanted a huge American flag suspended from the balcony beside the tree. On the tree, a white ribbon represented a ten dollar gift; a twenty-five dollars gift got a red ribbon; any gift over twenty-five dollars got a blue one.

The gifts were called Good Turns, and in exchange

my father was launching a new campaign the next Sunday, with a "one good turn deserves another" theme, tied in to the idea that that was the American way.

Earlier that morning I'd seen my father's scratch pad on his desk, where he was working on the sermon.

> *If you have an impossible dream, do a good turn, and see what happens to that dream.*
>
> *That's the American way! We're a country of buy one, get one free. We're a country that knows impossible dreams come true, because when you give it, you get it!*
>
> *"Give, and it shall be given unto you," it is written in Luke.*

I couldn't resist penciling in *"Thou hast thought that the gift of God may be purchased with money," it is written in Acts.*

Seal and I were starting the tree off with several hundred ribbons that were supposed to represent advance gifts from friends and neighbors. . . . It wasn't a total lie. Seal's family had made a $50 donation. Donald had tossed in $25. There were a few donations from the ACE staff, my mother, and our cook. The rest was bait.

("Bait?" my mother said. "Then so's the Golden Rule bait. If you like to think of it as a fishing expedition, then think of it as fishing lost souls out of dark waters. We're coming into peoples' homes to help them, not to frisk them.")

It was a warm, sunny afternoon with a little breeze and a quiet ocean. Seal and I were doing the bottom branches, stapling on the ribbons. Later I'd drive the ACE truck up beside the tree and do the top ones from the cherry picker.

Seal and I were talking back and forth while the ACE organist practiced inside The Summer House.

"They're doing a lot of kinky stuff down at The Hand," Seal said. "Arnelle tells my mother about it and my mother says she has all she can do to keep from asking her a hundred and one questions about it."

"What's wrong with asking a hundred and one questions?"

"Oh, Jesse, really. Someone says something to you like we're having a leg-growing session at the morning service, you just catch your breath and hope you'll get a few more facts—don't you know what I mean? It's like someone casually telling you God was in his bedroom the night before. I mean, you don't say, 'Oh, really, *where?*' It's too far out."

"Leg growing isn't all that kinky."

"Leg growing isn't all that kinky? *Leg* growing?"

"A lot of healers grow legs, or claim to."

"Okay," said Seal, "say that you're right. Say that there are a lot of healers who are leg growers. Say that's possible. Where do all these people come from with one leg shorter than the other?"

"They aren't so short you'd notice," I said. "Most healers claim a person's one leg is a third or a half inch shorter than the other. It's just something they say they see. They say it's what's causing backaches or bad feet—it's no big deal."

"Please spare me," Seal said. "All of that is a little too far out for me."

"You're probably right," I said. "Stick with more down-to-earth things like walking on water or parting the Red Sea."

Seal and I stood back from the pine tree and viewed our handiwork.

"We're heavy on white ribbons," I said.

"We're supposed to be," she said. "You discourage people if you make it look like everyone gives more than you can afford."

We took a break, stretched out on the lawn, and listened to an organ rendition of "Heaven's Sounding Sweeter."

In a pail next to us were the key ribbons I had to plant later, so that my father could pluck them from the tree the next Sunday, and read out an impossible dream. ("Here's a twenty-seven-year-old sweeper in an industrial plant whose impossible dream is going into business for himself. May the dream come true! It's—up—to—you!")

"Speaking of impossible dreams," Seal said, "why don't you kick in ten dollars and see if Opal will come to life at the Cheeks' party. She's so timid it's gross."

I said, "Here's a seventeen-year-old rich girl with her own sports car and her own swimming pool, whose impossible dream is that a sixteen-year-old girl without a pot to pee in will become socially acceptable overnight. May the dream come true! It's—up—to—you!"

"I'm not talking about socially acceptable," Seal said. "I'd just like to see her happy. It's super that you've asked her. I'd like to see you both happy."

"We'll manage," I said. I kept meaning to call Opal again, but I'd put it off. I could tell her father didn't like me calling, and it was hard to make conversation with her, too. The other thing was my preoccupation with what I kept telling myself couldn't be happening between Seal and Dickie.

Seal said, "Bud used to say she could be real pretty if she knew what to do with herself."

I was even glad when Bud's name came back into the conversation.

Seal said, "Bud loved telling me what I looked good in. He was always right."

"Bud was only wrong once," I said. "That was the time he thought he was wrong."

"The poor thing doesn't really know what to do with herself."

"Worry about you and Dickie," I said.

"Are you jealous of Dickie?" Seal chuckled. "I think you are." She rolled over on her stomach and rested her head on her arm. "I gave Opal some of my things, but I never see her in them."

"Maybe she's too embarrassed to wear them around you."

"She wasn't too embarrassed to take them."

"Maybe she wears them to Central High," I said. "I asked Opal because you wanted me to, now maybe you ought to get off her case."

"Maybe you've got the hots for her and won't admit it."

"Maybe it's you I've got the hots for," I said, and pounced on top of her, wrestling and laughing with her under the Good Turn Tree, rolling over finally to find my father glaring down at us.

He was dressed in Bermuda shorts, a Lacoste shirt and Top-Siders, fresh from his Sunday afternoon tennis game at The Hadefield Club. I started to make some crack about how I hoped he'd free the slaves so they could play games Sunday afternoons, too. But I decided that since Seal and I were rolling around on the lawn instead of working, it wouldn't go over big, and I decided, based on years of intimacy with him, there was something waiting to be unleashed after he gave one of his tight, little, polite smiles to Seal.

"Jesse, I'd like a word with you. Alone."

He began to look like a human bomb about to take off and turn into a mushroom cloud.

Seal whispered, "I bet he got beat again."

My father was notoriously lousy at sports. Much as he tried to be the kind of good old boy Donald was encouraging him to be, he was about as at home in locker rooms, along fairways, and on tennis courts as I was in poolrooms or pornographic bookstores.

We took a walk together down the path through the elephant grass, toward our house.

He said, "On the night of The Last Dance, I want you to make a presentation of five hundred dollars to The Ladies' Association from ACE. The town suffers the crowds we draw. One good turn deserves another."

"Yes, sir," I said. "Is that what you wanted to tell me?"

He didn't answer my question. He said, "I'm arranging to have a place for you on the program. You'll make a short speech of gratitude."

"Yes, sir."

Then he took a deep breath and let it out. "You'll never be Bud," he said finally. "Bud did things with love. But *you*, Jesse."

"Me what?"

"Don't try to imitate your brother, that's my advice. Don't try to take your brother's place. Find your own place."

I looked up at the brightly colored kites flying in the sky above the beach, squinting at the sun, beginning to feel the edge of anger move in closer to my gut. I said, "Seal and I were just horsing around . . . sir. . . . Did you ever just horse around?"

"Sometimes I think I horsed around all the time, where you're concerned," he said. "I'm not talking about the scene I just happened upon. I'm not dense enough to think Seal would change her loyalty from Bud to you."

"Thanks for that one," I said.

"You can attack, but I can't," he said. "And I don't. Not the way you do."

"What are you so damn mad at?" I said. "*Sir?*"

"I'm damned mad because you're damned vicious. Bud criticized my work because he thought he knew better ways to do it. You just go for the jugular. You just scribble something across my notes because you're a smart ass, not because you give a damn about me or ACE. Bud gave a damn!"

"If Bud had written that on your sermon pad, you would have laughed it off. Sir."

"Probably. Because it would have come from love, or it would have come from hate. But it wouldn't have come from indifference. It was just an indifferent, smark-aleck wisecrack!"

He stopped walking in the middle of the path and looked down at me.

"When did you change your mind about me?" he said. "Or did you always think I was just a money-grabbing crook?"

I suppose he had every right to be steamed, but I

wished just once he'd give it to me, without a testimony to my brother first.

"You called it right," I said with a mild shrug, determined not to let it build into the kind of brawl he and Bud went in for. "It *was* just a smart-aleck wisecrack."

But I'd thought about saying: When did you change your mind about being a preacher, or did you always think you ought to be a TV star?

He looked down at the ground. "Maybe I'm touchy, son, because I don't like certain things I have to do myself." Then he looked up and gave me one of those little smiles he pulled on camera, right before he made some kind of confession about how hard it was to ask for money, how much it was against his nature. (A week didn't go by they didn't flash the 800 numbers, and the "Call in your contribution" sign following them.)

He said, "This TV business is like a bottomless pit, Jesse. It was a lot simpler in the old days. We just passed the plate."

I could have said a lot back before he trotted down to the house to mix his martini before dinner, but I decided to shove it. I said, "It's not your fault, Dad."

He said that wasn't what he wanted to hear, really, and I raised my hand and let it drop in a gesture of helplessness, because it wasn't what I wanted to say, really.

Then he clapped one hand around my shoulder, hugged me, and got even in his own way, calling me Bud by accident, as he gave his usual end-of-conversation benediction. "I love you, son. I love you, Bud."

Then he corrected himself. "Jesse."

He feinted an embarrassed little punch near my chin, and I tried to let him off the hook by laughing hard with him.

Eleven

OPAL RINGER

"Here's a twenty-seven-year-old sweeper in an industrial plant whose impossible dream is going into business for himself! May the dream come true! It's up to you!"

"God Bless America" was playing softly in the background while Jesse's father reached out from the balcony to take another ribbon off The Good Turn Tree.

"He's a good showman, I'll give him that," Brother Dudley said, running his palm across his bald head, a glass of Flavor-Aid in his other hand, as he lay back in Daddy's Barcalounger, with his feet up in the air. "He's right up there with P. T. Barnum or the Ringling Brothers."

"If you like circuses," Daddy said. "They were circus people. . . . Oh, I admit, I admit, Guy Pegler's got more tricks up his sleeve than a hound dog's got fleas in August."

"Well, we got some tricks up our sleeves, too, Royal. We just got to learn to let people know about them."

"We got no tricks. We got The Power, that's what we got to let people know. I'm going to get in my van and go up and down the streets of this town, and the next town, and the next one after that. I'm aiming for five hundred people on our Saturday Soaking." He shot me a look. "Including you, Opal."

"I know including me," I said.

Daddy was still sitting at the card table, where they'd finished dividing up the offering from the morning service at The Hand. Brother Dudley'd grown six legs and they'd split three hundred dollars, but Daddy said there'd likely be more coming in next Wednesday night, once word got out Brother Dudley'd be back then. Daddy said pray God there'd be more on the way, because we were in debt up to our necks now. It was the reason for the Saturday-night Soaking, a twenty-four hour prayer/healing session to "help The Hand help the Lord help you." . . . Bobby John had his own idea to drag Guy Pegler to a memorial service for Willard Peyton, said Dr. Pegler owed Willard that much, and he'd be a drawing card, likely donate some of the money he got from Willard. (Daddy'd said it was a dumb idea and Bobby John went off to Drive-In Burger in a snit, to work the afternoon shift.)

Mum was making macaroni and cheese in the kitchen for dinner. We'd brought Brother Dudley back from The Hand to eat with us, and turned on the TV to watch Guy Pegler while we were waiting for Mum to get everything ready.

"Opal here's seeing his son," said Daddy.

"I'm not seeing him much," I said.

"She's got a date with him," said Daddy.

"So you said, so you said," Brother Dudley answered. "My own little girl married herself a salesman of sporting goods, moved over to Buffalo, New York."

"So you said," Daddy said. He was wearing the black coat with the silver lining I liked best of his coats, had his gray tie loosened.

"My little girl and her husband received The Power shortly after meeting, both at the same time, both slain in the spirit, reeling around like a pair of drunks it was such ecstasy."

"The ecstasy of the spirit," said Daddy. Brother

Dudley would shout it when he was healing: "The ecstasy of the spirit!"

I sat on the couch hugging a pillow, pushing my cuticles back to bring up my moons, and waiting for Mum to call in to me for help. She never did like anybody in her kitchen with her first thing when we got back from The Hand Sunday mornings. She was in there singing "God Bless America" very softly, rattling plates and pulling out the table leaves.

Daddy and Brother Dudley had their eyes fixed to the TV, and I was looking at it too, without seeing it, my thoughts running wild. I was thinking about Bobby John's secret meetings with Diane-Young. He'd say he was off to a Prayer-and-Share meeting down to Riverhead, then drive off to meet her somewhere.

"They did her over, Opal," he told me, "getting her ready for the Winning Rally. She don't look the same and's all painted like the Devil's lady. She don't talk the same, says I don't have an idea in my head except what's good and bad, says I can't ever come up with an in between."

"In between is Satan's wedge," I told him. "So Daddy says."

"So Daddy says."

He was going through a torment, I could tell, but he was still the only one I could talk to about being scared to go on my date with Jesse. I'd tell him boy was Jesse Pegler going to be sorry he ever asked me, because even if I did get my moons up, the rest of me was wanting, and I'd look so awful Jesse Pegler'd like to die carting me around. If I'd have told Daddy that, he'd lecture me on vanity, quote me Acts XIV:15, and if I'd have told Mum that, she'd say I was pretty as a picture and Jesse Pegler'd be proud to walk out with me anywhere. But Bobby John knew what I meant, said them and us was from two different worlds, and sometimes he got to thinking we wasn't the smart ones, they was; they had all the ideas.

Last night I kicked the covers off trying to sleep in the heat, and thinking about The Rapture. Daddy

was saying it was coming, he felt it, and Brother
Dudley was agreeing, saying, "Yes, it's on its way,"
while Daddy talked about a golden day going to be
here before we knew it.

When Mum kissed me good night in my room, I
asked her when she thought it'd come, this month,
this year? Would it come after the Soaking?

Mum said, "Oh, honey, it don't matter when, your
Daddy's so worried about a lot of things, he wants it
badly because we'll get our great reward then."

"I just wish the Soaking wasn't the same night as
The Last Dance," I said, "and sometimes I think
Daddy planned it that way."

"Daddy didn't plan it, Brother Dudley did. And
you got to make it to the Soaking, Opal," she said.

"I will. I said I would."

"You just pretend you're Cinderella at that dance
and you're going to leave it before your coach turns
into a pumpkin, hear?"

"I said I would."

"Daddy can't be asking folks to come if his own
family don't support it. You got half the evening to
dance, and then you come down to us."

"I said I would, I said I would, I said I would. But
I hate it. A lot. First time I ever got asked anywhere
important and I can't even stay to the end."

"Anything happens at The Hand's more important
than anything happens where you're going."

"I'm not telling them where I'm going, either. That's
all they'd need to hear. Opal Ringer's leaving The
Last Dance to go to a Soaking! They'd never let me
forget that one. I can hear them all now: Where'd
Opal go? Oh, Opal had to go to a Soaking."

"Opal Ringer," said Mum, "you think about them
too much. You think they think about you? You think
about them but they don't think about you, so now
you're lopsided, honey. You got to straighten yourself out."

"I know it."

Then I said, "What's ecstasy, Mum?"

"Ecstasy is what we're going to feel when The Rapture comes."

"But I looked it up in the dictionary, and rapture is ecstasy and ecstasy is rapture. I still don't know what it really means."

"They're words, honey. Words can't always say what things really mean."

"That's why they say it's unspeakable joy, I guess."

"If you get hot in here, you go down to the living room," Mum said, "sleep on the couch. You don't have enough breeze in here to lift lint off the windowsill. I'll tell you something, honey," she said, standing in the doorway, "there's a lot going on in your head coming up from your heart. It's like foreigners meeting and they don't speak the same language. They will, as you get older, but right now don't tire yourself trying to get all the answers."

For a time I lay in the dark singing to myself in a whisper, knowing how I'd sound if I would let the door of my heart come bursting open, come with a great light, lifting my words: *O Love divine, what hast Thou done! . . . Joy—bells ringing in your heart, joy bells ringing in your heart.*

When I did get to sleep, I saw the speck turn into me again, and felt the glow, and in the dream I told myself it wasn't a dream, that it was really real, then woke up sweating, a little of the glow left. It was like an old friend coming back, not to stay maybe, just to let me know there it was again.

"Opal," Daddy said, "stop mauling the pillow and go in and help your Mum!" He snapped off the TV. The show was over. He told Brother Dudley he had some praying to do, said help yourself to the Sunday paper or whatever you got in mind.

Brother Dudley had out a nail file, nodded, said, "I stopped reading the newspapers when I found Jesus, there's so little of Him anywhere in them. Don't worry about me, Royal."

In the kitchen, Mum was cutting up leftover ham

she'd brought down from the von Hennigs' last night, tossing it into the macaroni casserole.

I peeked into the bag the ham came out of and said, "What they throw out anyone could eat for a week on."

"Praise God," Mum said, "and thanks to them there's some real good licorice candy in there, Opal. There's cake I'll take to The Hand to have with coffee Wednesday night, cut it up in little pieces. Honey, have yourself some of that good licorice."

"It's you likes licorice."

"I don't care one way or the other."

"With all the Good & Plenty you eat?"

"I just like the name," Mum said.

Then Daddy started praying from in his room, same as he always did Sunday mornings, loud enough for the cat to hear sleeping way out on the roof of the van, even though Brother Dudley was right there in our living room.

"There he goes," I groaned.

"He's got every right," Mum said.

What bothered me wasn't his praying aloud. It was what he prayed about. It was like on Sundays he just got everything off his chest about us, told the Lord things he never told us face to face. We had to listen to all the things we'd done (no way we couldn't hear every blessed word) that sat heavy on his head like a basket of wet wash.

Doing it with Brother Dudley in the next room was like going to the toilet with the door open, in front of company.

Right away he started in on me, too.

". . . and I pray, Lord, that my daughter, Opal, will cast her eyes away from this godless astrology she's got herself interested in, to go to some dinner party or other. Let Your light shine on her, revealing the true stars in Your heavenly sky! Lead her to Your side at our Soaking, fill her with Your love at our Soaking, so she will know the only true dancing is dancing in the spirit, in Your name, never mind last dancing and last dances. Only the Lord has the last dance!"

I got so mad I began slamming dishes down on the table, while I was helping Mum set up for lunch.

Mum put her hand on my wrist to stop me making so much noise, said, "He don't mean it."

"He means it. He begrudges me anything everyone else does."

"He don't begrudge you it, he just don't want your head so turned, not by those people."

". . . and forgive me the sin of envy," Daddy continued. "I should have known better than your servant Guy Pegler how Willard loved that dog. I should have listened, and for not listening now I have the sin of envy. Someone else was rewarded for an act of kindness I did not extend!"

"I told him he should have took that dog," I said to Mum.

"Honey, don't be hard on him. We would have found Yellow a home. Willard wasn't dead yet. Don't you see how Guy Pegler's squeezing the breath out of your daddy? Takes his healing, takes Willard's money, and his son takes you off."

"I'm still here far as I know," I said.

"Lord, don't let me be too impatient with Bobby John, and forgive me for losing my temper over his stupid idea to bring Guy Pegler to a memorial service for Willard, for it that is Your wish, so be it. Seems like we're hurting too bad at The Hand for such turn-the-other-cheek ventures as carting Pegler down to a small service in Willard's memory, but Bobby John never was one to think past his nose, how well I know it!"

"At least Bobby John got his way for once," I said to Mum.

"Let up on your daddy, honey. He means well."

We had the ice cubes in the water glasses by the time he got to her.

". . . and Jesus, help Arnelle fight Satan's glut-

tony so's she can sing Your praises once again before
our humble flock, guide her from—"

"Gluttony?" Mum said, her face bright red.

"Shoe's on the other foot now," I said.

The memorial service for Willard Peyton was set
for noon on the day of The Last Dance.

Daddy was letting Bobby John be in charge of it,
since Daddy had other fish to fry. Fried them right
across from St. Luke's church, a moment after the
noon whistle blew.

Mrs. Bunch had closed down to go to the service,
and I'd decided to catch the bus back to Hog Creek
Road from Main Street, so I could pass by St. Luke's
and see them getting ready for the dance.

I didn't know anything about Daddy's plans. I was
walking along thinking about how people in that town
brought clothes in for cleaning that weren't even
dirty, trousers with the creases still in them, and
blouses wrinkled from being tucked in, but spotless.
That's what amazed me. I was trying not to think too
much about that night, and me being with all the
ones who took clean clothes in to be cleaned, but
feeling the little leap in my heart when I got to the
churchyard and saw the workers setting up everything. They were hoisting up a huge red-white-and-
blue-striped tent, with a wooden platform for dancing.
Women were cutting honeysuckle branches from
bushes on the ground, and men were stringing Jap-
anese lanterns from tree to tree.

The noon whistle gave me this punch of shock, it
sounded so loud. I was recovering from that jump to
my insides when I heard Daddy's voice, big as all
outdoors, and twice as powerful.

"SINNERS? WHERE ARE YOU GOING TO-
NIGHT, AND WHEN YOU GET THERE, WHAT
ARE YOU GOING TO DO, AND WHEN YOU DO
IT, WHAT IS IT GOING TO MEAN?

"IF YOU'RE COMING TO THE HELPING HAND
TABERNACLE, WHEN YOU GET THERE YOU'RE

GOING TO PRAY, YOU'RE GOING TO BE HEALED, YOU'RE GOING TO RECEIVE CHRIST AS YOUR PERSONAL SAVIOR, YOU'RE GOING TO FEEL THE POWER ... AND IT'S GOING TO MEAN YOU'RE NEW, YOU'RE SAVED, YOU'RE SAFE, YOU MADE IT, YOU'RE BORN AGAIN!"

Everyone around me just froze, same as I did.

I could see the van parked across the street, speakers up on the roof.

"SINNERS? WHERE ARE YOU GOING TO-NIGHT, WHO ARE YOU GOING WITH, WHO ARE YOU GOING TO SEE?

"OH, I GOT OTHER PLANS, YOU SAY, I HAVEN'T GOT TIME TO GET SAVED, YOU SAY, I'D GET SAVED, YOU SAY, IF I DIDN'T HAVE TO GO SOMEWHERE FOR A PARTY, YOU SAY, IF I COULD ONLY GET AWAY, YOU SAY, IF I DIDN'T HAVE TO GO TO A DANCE, YOU SAY, IF I COULD ONLY SQUEEZE THE LORD JESUS CHRIST INTO MY SCHEDULE, YOU SAY, AND YOU ARE DAMNED!"

"Royal Ringer," a woman near me said to another, and she laughed.

"It's not funny. It's disgusting," said the other woman. "It's disgraceful!"

"YOU NEED TO COME TO THE TWENTY-FOUR-HOUR SOAKING AT THE HELPING HAND TABERNACLE, YOU NEED TO BE SOAKED WITH THE SPIRIT, YOU NEED TO BE SOAKED WITH LOVE, YOU NEED TO BE SOAKED WITH LIGHT, YOU NEED TO BE SOAKED WITH GLORY! YOU NEED, YOU NEED, YOU NEED JE-SUS! YOU NEED JESUS!"

"I don't need *this*," someone said.

I didn't either, and I walked away fast, breaking into a run, finally, heading down Main with Daddy's voice chasing me: "YOU NEED, YOU NEED, YOU NEED, YOU NEED JE-SUS! I SAID JE-SUS. I SAID JE-SUS CHRIST YOUR LORD AND SAV-IOR!"

* * *

By the time I got home, the Seaville Police had made Daddy stop, said Seaville had a noise ordinance. Mum said when it came to Daddy they had a noise ordinance; what about all the noise every Sunday morning, traffic pouring in for *It's Up to You*, horns going, what about all that noise?

I was so down in the dumps I was hardly hearing her rave, sitting in my rocker in my room, rocking my body, rocking my head from side to side like I was watching a tennis match and not just feeling the shame of being me, hugging my arms in my undies.

Mum finally took notice of my condition, said, "You been waiting for tonight all your life, now look at you. Face down to the floor like you was going to a funeral."

"You don't know anything," I said. "Daddy downtown calling everyone sinners through loudspeakers, and I got to face the whole bunch of them tonight."

"Daddy's got a right."

"You always take his side," I said.

"It's Daddy's business to call people sinners, honey. That's the business Daddy's in."

"I got to face the whole bunch of them and I'm the only one can't wear a hat."

"Confounded be all they that serve graven images, the Bible says."

"Pisces isn't a graven image," I said, "it's a sign of the zodiac. I'm going to be the only one there without a hat. Why don't the Bible say something about that?"

"Hush now. Shush! You should be counting your blessings right now, not looking for the hole in the doughnut."

"I know it," I said, "but seems like I never will be one of them, not even for one little night."

"I love the way Jesus' eyes is always following you in this room," said Mum, looking at the picture Bobby John gave me. "I'd rather belong to Jesus any day than belong to that crowd."

"I don't know as we got a choice," I said.

"I tell you what, honey!" Mum said. "Play your radio, and bring out everything you're going to wear, and what we'll have is a dress rehearsal. Now, what are you going to wear? Let's get it all out on the bed."

"My lemon-yellow dress," I said. "Oh, Mum, I'm real scared."

"Nothing to be scared about. Get that dress out, honey." She snapped on the radio. "When he comes, I'll answer the door and then you'll come down. That's how it's done."

"When I hear that doorbell," I said, getting out of my rocker, "I'm going to climb right into my bed and pull the covers over my head!"

There was a sweet song coming through the radio. Mum was laughing. "You're going to wait right up here until I shout up at you, 'Your young man's here, Opal!' "

The color came to my neck and spread up across my face. "You shout he's my young man up to me and I'll never come down!" I said. "Now, I swear I won't, Mum! You got to promise me you won't shout nothing like that up those stairs!"

She was giggling and getting me to giggling, when the song coming through the radio stopped in the middle, and the announcer said there was a bulletin.

"A bulletin!" Mum said.

". . . repeat, a bulletin," the announcer said. "Dr. Guy Pegler has been abducted by an unknown kidnaper. Dr. Guy Pegler has been—"

"What's abducted?" I said.

Mum said, "Shh! Listen!"

". . . while he was on his way from a local church service. The Pegler family was informed he's being held hostage. There are no other details at this moment."

"Honey," Mum said, "we got to get down on our knees."

Twelve

JESSE PEGLER

The morning of The Last Dance, my mother and Seal and I worked on ACORN applications.

When Mrs. Davison, our housekeeper, announced that lunch would be served in fifteen minutes, my mother said, "Seal, honey, you'll stay for a bite to eat, won't you? Donald's staying."

"I can't," Seal said. She was working in white short shorts, and a yellow cotton sweater the color of her hair, with a thin belt around it. "Dickie and I are going to work on our hats, so I'm having lunch at the Clowards'."

"Are you up to all that excitement?" I said. I'd intended to sound cool, but my voice cracked mid-sentence. I think Seal noticed how weird I sounded, because she didn't zing me back.

"You go along, dear," said my mother. "You worked with Diane-Young yesterday, didn't you? How's she coming?"

"She's finally got the removable braces," Seal said, unwinding her long, tan legs, getting to her feet, "but the contact lenses aren't working. They irritate her eyes. She'll have to go back to her regular glasses."

"Not those pink things?" my mother said.

"Those pink things," Seal said. "But I've been teaching her about makeup, and *quelle change!* The only thing is, she says s-h-i-blank every other word—or crappy—and she's not too believable as a witness. Her eyes blink madly whenever she talks about the healing."

"Oh, I'm not worried about Diane-Young," my mother chirped. "The Cheeks are so delighted she's going on the Winning Rally! You'll get her into shape. You and Dickie are doing wonders with her."

"How'd Dickie get in on the act?" I asked. It was news to me.

"He wants to help"—Seal shrugged—"so he's helping."

"Why not?" my mother said. "Nothing going on with the Methodists, and he's an enthusiastic young man. The more the merrier, I say."

"Anyway"—my mother began one of her old familiar refrains—"ACE's aim is to form a coalition with local churches, all working together, with the same goal, to spread the Lord's—"

Et cetera, et cetera, while I watched Seal comb her long blond hair and pull down her sweater after. I smelled her perfume. I remembered nights Bud would come back from dates with her, that same smell was on his clothes.

As soon as Seal left my mother's office, my mother whispered across at me, "I think they've got a thing going on."

"Dickie Cloward's my age," I said. That was getting to be my own old familiar refrain.

"I always said a girl like Seal isn't going to wait around forever."

"You don't have to whisper, Mom, there's no one here but us chickens."

"Let that be a lesson to Bud."

"If Bud wanted her back, all he'd have to do would be show up. That thing would be *pfft*."

"I wonder," my mother said.

I was beginning to wonder myself. I found myself looking past my mother, out the picture window, where Seal was walking down the path from our house. The wind was blowing her hair, and she was taking these long steps as though she was in a big hurry.

I watched her until she was out of sight.

My mother began gathering up her papers. "Don't think I've forgotten about your hat, darling." I was planning to wear a derby to The Last Dance, with two ears of corn attached to it, representing Virgo's harvest. "I'm going to fix it for you right after lunch," my mother said.

"Thanks, Mom. I love you, sir."

She laughed. "I love you, too," she said. "I just wish your father and I could go to that thing tonight."

"So do I. Then I wouldn't have to make a speech."

"Your father's right, I guess. It's fine if we go to the Cheeks' dinner, but we'd be too big a distraction at St. Luke's." She went across the room and picked up Blanche. "It wouldn't be fair to The Ladies' Association. Remember how your father got mobbed at Rotary's Las Vegas night?"

She held the cat up to her face and let out a long sigh. "Seems like can't go wins out over can go about ten to one these days," she said. "Blanche, here, gets out more than I do."

At lunch Donald sawed a piece of rare roast beef and announced that the Lord was suggesting to my father that ACE ought to take the Winning Rally to England.

"Guy included?" my mother said.

Donald said, "It wouldn't make much sense to go over there without our star attraction."

"I wonder where our star attraction is?" my mother said, glancing at her watch.

"He's probably signing autographs," Donald said. "He'll be along. . . . I remember reading about Billy Graham's first crusade beyond America. It was in 1954."

"I don't like ACE going over there," my mother said.

"Anyway," Donald went on, "Billy got himself in-

vited to Windsor Castle for tea with the Queen."
Donald swallowed a chunk of roast beef and chuckled,
anticipating the story he was determined to tell.

"What happened was"—another chuckle, another
chunk of beef—"Billy strolled in and grabbed this
fellow's hand—fellow was in tails, white gloves—and
Billy said, 'Honored to meet you, sir.' Well, this
fellow turned out to be the butler. He just wanted to
take Billy's hat."

My mother wasn't that amused. She said, "Where
are we going to get the money to go to England?"

"We'll raise it," Donald said. "We'll get it back over
there. There's a whole new resource to tap over
there. . . . The Lord will provide."

"Is the Lord suggesting this or are you suggesting
this?" my mother said.

"The Lord made the motion and I seconded it,"
said Donald.

I said, "All in favor say aye. . . . Nay."

"Nay," my mother said. "When and where do we
stop? I read where Billy Graham's hardly ever home.
Television is one thing, traipsing all over the globe is
another thing."

"What do you think, Jesse?" Donald asked.

"I already said nay. Enough is enough."

"Is enough," my mother said. "Amen."

Donald's mouth was open and he was ready to say
something, when Mrs. Davison came into the dining
room.

She said the Seaville Police were on the phone.

"Well, what do they want?" Donald said, and a
hunk of roast beef fell off his fork.

My mother was on her feet.

By two that afternoon, network news was report-
ing my father's kidnapping. The Cheeks canceled their
dinner party. We all waited for the police to contact
Bobby John Ringer, to get more details of what happened after the memorial service.

All we knew was that my father's kidnaper would

announce his demands sometime that evening, returning my father safely when they were met.

We had extra police added to our security force, and Donald was busy on one of our phones seeing what assets he could transfer to cash.

There was nothing to do but wait, and my mother and I sat together in my father's study.

We prayed, we tried to play a game of backgammon, we listened to the radio announcements.

Finally my mother just broke down and cried, and talked about the old days, not just our days under the tent, but when she was a child, out on the evangelical trail with my grandfather, Reverend Jesse Cannon.

"I wasn't very different from that poor little girl you were taking to the dance tonight."

"Opal."

"Only my daddy wouldn't have let me go."

"I don't think her daddy was too thrilled about her going."

"Mine wouldn't have let me. Did you call her, honey?"

"She said she'd been praying for Daddy. Her and her mother."

"Did she know any more about what took place down there?"

"I told you, Mom. She doesn't know any more than we do."

"They're so emotional sometimes, those people. Emotional, resentful deep down, oh, I don't blame them."

"It might not have even been one of them."

"I used to hate it when anyone from a better class came to our services."

"I know. Me too."

"Like they were sightseeing. . . . I couldn't even go to dances at school—my daddy would hit the ceiling if you said 'dance' to him. . . . The first time I ever danced was on my wedding night. I stepped all over your father's shiny new shoes. . . . Maybe this is a sign, Jesse."

"It's a sign of the times."

"I don't mean a sign of the times. I mean a sign from the Lord."

"I know what you mean."

"You don't believe He sends signs." It wasn't a question.

"I don't know what I believe anymore," I said.

"Anymore? You never did know, darling. That's why it never tugged at you the way it did at Bud. Even when you were little boys, you were as different as day and night. Bud was a terror. I never knew what he'd do next—even when his little legs first started walking, they walked toward trouble. . . . You were my good boy."

"Little Goody Two-shoes," I said.

"You weren't a Goody Two-shoes, but you weren't the little devil Bud was. Bud was always hiding from your father over something he did. He always dreaded your father coming home, finding out. Remember how he used to just skip out before dinner because he knew he was in for it?"

"Yeah. I remember."

"Your father'd say let him go hungry. Later on I'd sneak some dinner up to him, unbeknownst to your father."

"I don't know how unbeknownst it was to him."

My mother gave a sad little chuckle. "Maybe it wasn't so unbeknownst. Your father saw himself in Bud."

"The more things change, the more they stay the same."

"Oh, I know you think he loves Bud more, it isn't that. He just knows Bud better. Bud's familiar. He's going through what your father went through, what his father went through, what my father went through. The anger, the doubting, everything you go through when the Lord is testing you."

"I guess I never felt He was testing me."

"You never really let Him into your life to find out."

"Oh, Mom."

"Well? You don't seem to require very much he... You seem to have your passions under control. You don't feel the temptations, the pull between good and bad. You don't think the Lord sends signs. You don't think what's happening right now to your father could be a sign to us."

"I think we've been talking so much about money every single Sunday, we've put ideas into someone's head."

"And I think," my mother said, "the Lord is telling us to pull back!"

Donald Divine walked into my father's study then.

"Well, we know who our kidnaper is now," he said. "He's Bobby John Ringer."

That night on CBS, NBC, and ABC, a photograph was shown of Bobby John.

For some reason he was holding up a small, three-legged footstool, probably something he'd made himself, because he had this proud grin on his face, and he was holding it with one hand, pointing at it with the other.

It was one of those blurred, candid shots that didn't blow up well, and didn't tell you anything but what you saw: this very tall, lean fellow in dark pants, and a white shirt with the sleeves rolled up, the wind blowing his black hair up from the top of his head.

The newsmen were doing their usual bit, playing it up big, taking every little thread of information concerning Bobby John and trying to spin it into something. They were waiting for a tape to come of Bobby John's telephone conversation with the Seaville police.

They were describing Bobby John as "a loner," "not very prepossessing," one newsman said he was reported to have "a curious shuffling walk, and an odd vacuous smile." Another newsman described him as "nondescript" and "separated from the mainstream by his religious fanaticism."

"It's easy to see," one commentater said, "why a socially isolated young man with almost archaic religious beliefs—a loser, in other words—might resent the powerful, successful, magnetic TV evangelist, Dr. Guy Pegler—champion of winners!"

Just before the seven-o'clock newscasts were ending, Bobby John's voice came crackling across the airwaves:

"Dr. Pegler is safe. All I'm asking for is equal time to correct a situation. D. Y., I'd like you to be with me. She knows who she is. D. Y., we're both in this thing together. . . . We both want to get something off our chests so's we don't bear false witness no more. Anymore.

"I'm not blaming Dr. Pegler or *It's Up to You*, because it was all my idea, with Satan helping. There's a twenty-four hour Soaking at The Helping Hand Tabernacle tonight. That's as good a time as any to get this thing cleared up.

"I'll be there by ten o'clock and Dr. Pegler will be with me. D. Y., honeybunch, after this is all over I want you to be my wife. I'm asking you that on network TV. If you'll have me.

"Come to the Soaking in The Hollow at The Helping Hand Tabernacle. This sinner will be there. . . . And thank you, Jesus. . . . I hope I've got a good 10-2. 10-10."

Thirteen

OPAL RINGER

Right after we heard Bobby John on the seven o'clock news, Daddy came in his van to take Mum, me, and the sandwiches we made for the Soaking to The Hand.

"Well," Daddy said, "he's done it this time! This time he's really done it up good!"

"Faking that thing was weighing on his brain just like a tumor," Mum said.

"What brain's that, I'd like to know," said Daddy. "He's the new overnight sensation's what he is, got himself a worldwide reputation now, in a class with Lee Harvey Oswald, Sirhan Sirhan, and John Hinckley. On the news driving over here, I heard he was a dangerous religious fanatic!"

"That's the killer!" Mum said.

"I said to Jesus coming over, Well he's Your boy now, if You still want him. I wash my hands of him."

"I don't and Jesus don't."

"Jesus don't wash His hands of anybody, is the only reason he don't wash His hands of Bobby John."

I swear Jesus made that summer night Himself, too. Driving along between them in the front seat of the van, I never saw so many stars show themselves before the sky got dark, while the sun was still going down, and in the warm evening air, all the sweet smells of things coming to blossom.

Late that afternoon when word came it was only

Bobby John holding Guy Pegler, I still had the hope like some soft tiny baby bird's feather rustling around in the wind we'd go to that dumb dance, thought Jesse might call back, say, Well, it's only your brother, so no sense spoiling everything we looked forward to, Opal.

While I looked out the window of the van at the town, I knew that town so well, tears started leaking out of my eyes.

"Hush, now, honey," Mum said, "you'll get your pretty yellow dress all salty tears."

"I never thought I'd be wearing this thing just to a Soaking," I said.

"How are the Peglers taking it?" Daddy said.

"They're not coming to The Hand," I said. "They're going to let the police handle it. Jesse's staying home with his mother."

"I said how are they taking it, not what are they doing?"

"They're just taking it," I said. (Jesse? I told him, I'm real disappointed about the dance, *real* disappointed. Yeah, he said back. Well, Opal, we can't stay on the phone now.)

"They shouldn't come to The Hand, they're right about that. Police got roadblocks up, traffic's thicker than Hell's crowds with Satan's sightseers."

"Are our own people getting through?" Mum said.

"They're there, most of them by now, with the cameras and the newsmen. I said we'll have no cameras in the church, that was my first thought, but Brother Dudley said let them set up, won't hurt the unsaved to see the saved one little bit, won't hurt anyone to see a real church and not a nightclub act."

"Still no word from Bobby John?" Mum said.

"Nothing you didn't hear on the TV. Says he's coming, bringing Guy Pegler with him. Well, the police are waiting. So's his girl friend."

"D. Y.'s there?" I said.

"Seems she's changed herself into a girl from whatever she was before."

"She was always a girl, Royal. That's what got Bobby John into all this trouble."

"Well she's there, with her daddy, and more police."

"What got Bobby John into all this trouble was he was trying to help The Hand," I said. "You don't know anything."

"I know The Hand could do without his help," Daddy said.

When we got down into The Hollow, the police stopped the van to check it out, then let us on through.

Brother Dudley was conducting the service. Daddy'd told him we were all just going on with the Soaking, never mind Bobby John's crazy schemes. Daddy went in the back door of The Hand, while Mum and I took the sandwiches down to the basement.

We could hear them upstairs, stamping their feet and shouting through Brother Dudley's words, and the organ playing softly, playing my favorite:

> *Take the Savior here below*
> *With you everywhere you go.*
> *He will keep the joy bells ringing in your heart . . .*
> *Joy—bells, ringing in your heart.*

"Well," Mum said when we got finished putting out paper plates and napkins, "we'd better go on up, honey. Whatever will happen will happen."

She gave me a hug. "You look so pretty in that dress, honey."

"Thanks to Bobby John it don't matter what I look like in any dress," I said. "He's just like Daddy, only thinks about himself."

"Who're you thinking about but your own self, Opal Ringer?"

"He could have picked another time is all I'm saying."

"People don't pick the time they go off their rocker, honey," said Mum. "Bobby John isn't in his right mind. . . . That won't be the last Last Dance, anyway."

"For me it is," I said. "I'm back in the same old rut."

She put her arm around me and we walked toward the stairs. "Don't be worrying about ruts, sweetheart," she said. "When The Rapture comes—"

I didn't even let her finish. "That dumb thing isn't ever coming! We just always say it's coming when we can't take what's already here!"

But Mum was going right on anyway, ". . . the door will open in heaven and the first voice will be as a trumpet talking, saying, Come up hither. . . ."

There is a time to everything, I've known that to be true.

A time to be born, and a time to die, as the Bible tells it; a time to plant, and a time to pluck up that which is planted; A time to kill, and a time to heal; a time to break down . . . which is what happened to Bobby John's car that night, with Guy Pegler in it.

Sometimes I get to wondering what that night would have been like if that hadn't happened to his car, and if he had made it to The Hand. But wondering that way, I've learned, doesn't mean anything, because the meaning in everything is in what really happened, not in what might have happened.

What really happened was the police found them broken down, three miles from The Hollow, on Tanning Hide Road. They took Bobby John in; they took Guy Pegler home.

In between that happening and our finding out about it, my whole life changed. During that inbetween time, long after the seed time, was the harvest, and I'll tell you this about those harvests from my own experience: You don't see them coming. That's what amazes me.

Brother Dudley'd been on for hours without one leg growing, and no visible healing. It was the lights of the cameras making people reluctant, Daddy said when we stopped for sandwiches, and the strangers among us, so many faces unfamiliar to us, newspeople and people sneaking in, claiming they were always at them things. It was the restlessness in the crowd, everyone watching the door, waiting for Bobby John and Dr. Pegler. The air was too charged up, Daddy said, the only thing to do was go in the same direction.

Daddy went on at the stroke of ten, wearing his silver-lined coat, jumping suddenly like an exclamation point turning into a comma while he shouted at them: "SINNNNN—NERS!"

Crouched down, his fist in his palm where he'd punched it.

A silence that sent a chill up your spine.

Whispered next, soft but like the sissing sound of a rattle on a big snake's tail: "Sinners. . . . What are you here for?" a little louder, "Why did you come here?" and louder, "WHAT ARE YOU DOING HERE?"

You could feel people's hearts beating, feel everything stopped but the heartbeats, and the red eye of the TV camera.

"WHAT ARE YOU HERE FOR?"

"To get saved," someone.

"WHAT?"

"To get saved," more.

"WHAT? WHAT? WHAT? WHAT?"

"To get SAVED!"

"GOD!" Daddy shouted. "My high tower, and my refuge, and my Savior!"

"My high tower!" Mrs. Bunch called out.

"My HIGH tower!"—Daddy.

Then when I looked up, raising my hands and my eyes with everyone, while we shouted it out, I saw him.

Saw him on his long legs coming in the pew, tie hanging down, blue eyes seeing mine, squeezing past people until he was at my side.

Said, "Opal," leaning down, warm breath near my ear, then, "Hi."

"Bud," all I could manage.

"My HIGH tower!" Daddy shouted.

"My HIGH tower!"—everyone. Me. Bud.

"My REFUGE! My SAVIOR!"

"My REFUGE!"—everyone. Me. Bud. "My SAVIOR!"

Bud Pegler put his hands out, palms up to receive the spirit, shouted out, shouted, "Yes, Jesus!"

"YES, JESUS!"—others.

"JE-SUS!"—everyone.

"YES, JE-SUS!" everyone shouted.

Then I did. "Yes, Je-sus!"

We all were, and I knew something soon as we all were, with the organ starting, choir beginning softly:

"When love shines in,
How the heart is tuned to singing,

knew I belonged there and they were my own.

Knew he belonged there.

Even in the bright lights, in the camera's eye beaming out at us, when I saw Mum come down from the choir, that look in her eye, I felt my heart leap under my dress, but not the old wild fearful way now. My eyes couldn't get enough of her, loving her thick legs moving side to side that way, beginning, loving her fat arms reaching up, listening to her, watching her big, sweet body swaying, Bud's body swaying beside my own, everyone moving back and forth, music lifting us up, swaying back and forth. I was going up so high. I was on a climb. I was reaching so high that suddenly Bud's hand reached high to grab mine, holding mine but not able to keep me down until I fell.

I fell.

I don't know how long I was down. Mum said not that long, but I came up singing.

I came up and I was singing, the way I'd always thought I could, just as loud and not in any language that I ever heard before, just as loud and in my own voice, soaking wet all over me, cameras going, I could see their red eyes on me, tiny red living specks, and I had tongues. I felt my body giving room to my soul while it burst into full bloom.

Bud Pegler drove me home, while Daddy and Mum went down to bail out Bobby John. The Soaking was still going on.

"It was worth coming home to hear you, Opal," Bud said.

We were coming up from The Hollow in the starry night.

"Well, it just happened."

"Yes, God. It happened."

"But I never thought my own brother would do a thing like that."

"If I'd known it was Bobby John, I don't think I'd have come all the way from Connecticut ninety miles an hour." He looked at me, smiling, the whitest teeth. "I'm glad I did now."

"What were you doing there?"

"I was working at a nursery, landscaping, gardening. I was having all these arguments in my head with my father."

"Daddy and Bobby John are always arguing, too."

"Ever since my father got on TV, we haven't gotten along well. I have trouble with the TV part of his ministry, I guess."

"I'll tell you one thing," I said. "After a while you don't even notice you're on camera."

Bud laughed real hard at that.

"Well, you don't," I said.

He reached down and snapped on the radio. He put his long arm on the back of the seat behind my head. I had my hands folded and could see the moons up on the nails of my right fingers. I let my head drop back, turned my cheek to the sleeve of his coat.

Some song came on, I don't know—one of them. We rode along without talking, tired and full in the spirit. I thought of me thinking of everyone going two by two past my window, thought of myself with nothing on but my panties, those hot nights back in my room, like the speck not knowing about the glow.

I finally knew all the truth about the glow, driving up from The Hollow in the summer night. No glow could ever be one if it didn't start off a speck.

That's what amazed me.

Fourteen

JESSE PEGLER

Near midnight my brother called to say that he was in Seaville, that he'd gone directly to The Helping Hand Tabernacle, and that he'd be home as soon as he dropped off Opal Ringer.

My father was already asleep in bed, exhausted from the ordeal with Bobby John. I'd just come back from making the ACE presentation at The Last Dance.

Mother and Donald decided to let my father sleep; he'd had too much excitement for one day. He had to be up early for *It's Up to You.*

I went up to my room, changed into my pajamas, and listened to the radio in the dark. When I heard my mother's whoop of joy downstairs, I knew Bud had come through the front door.

I got up and put on my robe.

I stalled around a little, waiting for the fireworks to end.

When I finally went down the staircase, he was still standing in the hall, his suitcase at his feet, somehow taller. He had on a suit and a shirt and a tie.

"Hey! Jesse!" he shouted up at me, and the next thing I knew I was trying to keep from bawling myself (tears were running down my mother's face; even Donald was teary eyed), and I was taking the steps by twos, running toward him.

"Jesse! Jesse!" And he hugged me hard.

We let go of each other and I gave him a punch on the arm, laughing up at him, our eyes meeting for the first time. He had this look on his face, familiar and not, and for a minute I just stared at him to try and figure out what there was about the look, until he said, "Thank you, Jesus." He shut his eyes. "Oh, thank you, Jesus," serious, a whisper, and I saw my father, the same way my father must have always seen himself, younger, yes, but it was unmistakably him.

After Donald left, I went back up to bed, to give my mother a chance to talk with Bud alone.

When he finally came into our bedroom, he talked as he undressed, small talk, checking to be sure our father really was okay, saying he was a little worried about Mother, she seemed down.

He was getting into his pajama bottoms when he finally said, "I was about ready to come home, anyway."

"To stay?"

"For a while."

"And then?"

"Then I might go to Western Bible Institute."

I didn't say anything.

"I'm bushed," he said.

I said so was I.

He didn't ask about Seal. He said it felt good to be back, he'd missed everyone, he'd watched *It's Up to You* every week.

"You were so close," I said. "Why didn't you just come home for a weekend if you missed everyone so much?"

He was sitting there bare chested, in his pajama bottoms, finishing a Marlboro, smoking the way he always had, no hands, the cigarette hanging out of the side of his mouth, smoke curling up past his face.

"I wanted to do a lot of thinking," he said.

Then he put out his cigarette and said, "Hey, let's get some sleep. Do you want to pray with me first?" and he was actually getting down on his knees.

I pretended to sleep late the next morning so my father and Bud could enjoy their reunion.

My father made the most of it. He got Bud to go on camera with him, and Bud stood in the receiving line with him after the service was over.

My mother and father and Bud had breakfast together after *It's Up to You,* and I straggled in after they were finished. My mother was in the kitchen, and Bud and my father were sitting over coffee.

". . . and you don't think Jesus would have taken advantage of television to get His message across?" my father was saying as I strolled into the dining room.

"Good morning," I said.

"I'm just saying I wouldn't want a television ministry," Bud said. "I'd be happy in a little church somewhere in the sticks."

"Good morning, son," said my father. ". . . Are you too good for television?"

"No, I'm not too good for it! Hi, Jesse."

"Pull up a chair, Jesse, son. . . . I asked you if you don't think Jesus would have taken advantage of television to get His message across?"

"I'm not talking about Jesus now," Bud said. "I'm talking about me."

"Me me me," my father said.

So nothing'd changed in that department.

I sat there and let them go at it.

After breakfast, Bud said he'd like to drive around Seaville.

"Does that sound good to you, Jesse?" he asked me.

I thought he probably wanted to get out of the house, get away from Dad. I gave him a wink and a smile and we took off.

On our way into town, I said, "I hate the tube, too. If you ask me, it's Dad's ego trip."

Bud said, "Well, he was right about Jesus. Jesus spoke to crowds whenever he could. There were thousands at the Sermon on the Mount."

I had nothing to say to that.

When we got to Seaville, we drove down Main Street, past St. Luke's, where workers were taking down the tent and the lights from The Last Dance.

I told him one of the reasons Mom might have seened "down" was she couldn't go to many things with Dad anymore. Dad always got mobbed. I told him how they'd decided not to go to the dance, and how disappointed Mom was.

"She doesn't have enough contact with people," Bud said.

"She runs ACORN," I said. "Seal helps her with it."

"ACORN is all done by correspondence," Bud said. "Mom likes the dinner on the ground, gather round kind of thing."

"Seal's helping her with ACORN," I said.

"I heard you the first time," Bud said. "I talked with Seal this morning. She's going with Dickie Cloward now."

I felt as if I was falling a long way down.

We drove from Main Street to Seaville High, and around the back to the stadium, where we parked for a while, and Bud smoked.

"I might skip Western Bible and stick around for a while."

"For Mom's sake," I said.

"Dad needs me, too."

"You'd work for ACE?"

"All ACE really is, is him," said Bud.

"And Donald."

"Yep."

"Don't forget Divine Donald," I snickered, and I looked across at Bud, but he wasn't picking up on the old cue.

He finally said, "I've missed Dad."

He didn't say me.

He didn't even say Mom.

He said he missed Dad.

Then he changed the subject. "Something really extraordinary happened at The Helping Hand Tabernacle last night," he began, and that was when I first heard about Opal.

It's been about six months now, and as Donald would say, she's the hottest ticket in town.

They come from far and wide to see Opal, and hear her sing in tongues. Since her one and only TV appearance the night of the Soaking, she's become the newest Seaville celebrity.

I haven't gone to see her. I don't think I will. It's not because I'm not curious. I am.

But for a while anyway, I'm not going to any church.

"Oh, now *you're* going through that stage," my mother says. "First Bud, now you."

My father doesn't say much, not to me, anyway. He's busy battling with Bud, the color back in his cheeks, and the sparkle in his eyes again. Sunday mornings they star together on the white balcony, in matching blue robes with gold tassels. You've probably seen them, and just before they come into view, you've probably seen

GUY PEGLER! GUY JR!

IT'S UP TO

　　　　YOU! GUY PEGLER GUY JR. IT'S UP TO

　　　　YOU you you you you you you

　　　　guy guy guy guy guy guy guy

　　　　guy jr. guy jr. guy jr. guy jr.

　　　　GUY　　　　　　　GUY JR.

　　　　　PEGLER AND

Next month the two of them are taking a Winning Rally to England and Australia.

"One day," my mother says, "your name will be up there with theirs."

I never tell her that's what I'm most afraid of.

Fifteen

OPAL RINGER

You all know the rest.

Bud often comes to hear me, says someday he hopes I'll be on one of their shows. He's not the only one who's asked me to go on the TV. I've been asked by famous TV shows besides *It's Up to You*, and I've been asked by people who've got nothing to do with the Lord, and offered money.

But I belong to The Helping Hand Tabernacle. You have to come down to The Hollow to hear me.

One time way far back, I made a wish on a cookie wrapper going up in flames, that you all'd really like me.

Now you come to hear me sing tongues, so many of you Daddy says it's like flies on the sweet cake. He has D. Y. and Bobby John down at the door, seeing we got room before we let you in.

We've got the CheckCheek installed now and Daddy does the offering with a computer.

You all come but him. Jesse doesn't come.

Bud says, "He's lost, we have to pray for Jesse, Opal," and it's something we can do together without getting into trouble. Me and him has seen the Devil's face, sweet nights when we slip, for there's the sin in us same as there's the spirit.

If I was to say that finally Opal Ringer was going

to tell you what she really thinks of you, would you laugh?

I love you, yes I love you. When The Rapture comes, I want you all along, somehow, someway, every last one of you, ascending with me.

When The Rapture comes, I hope you're there.

I know all your faces so well.

About the Author

M. E. Kerr was born in Auburn, New York, attended the University of Missouri, and now lives in East Hampton, New York. Ms. Kerr is the author of several novels for young people, including DINKY HOCKER SHOOTS SMACK! and IF I LOVE YOU, AM I TRAPPED FOREVER?

JOIN THE SIGNET **VISTA READER'S PANEL**

Help us bring you more of the books you like by filling out this survey and mailing it in today!

1. The title of the last paperback book I bought was:
   _____

2. Did someone recommend this book to you?
   (Check One) ☐ Yes ☐ No
   If YES, was it a ☐ Friend ☐ Teacher ☐ Librarian ☐ Parent.
   If NO, did you choose it because of: ☐ the cover ☐ the autho
   ☐ the subject ☐ other: _____

3. Would you recommend this book to someone else?
   (Check One) ☐ Yes ☐ No

4. How many paperback books have you bought for your own
   reading enjoyment in the last six months?
   ☐ 1 to 3 ☐ 4 to 6 ☐ 7 to 10 ☐ 11 to 15 ☐ 16 or more

5. I usually buy my books at (Check One or more):
   ☐ Bookstore ☐ Drug Store ☐ Dept. Store ☐ Supermarket
   ☐ Discount Store ☐ School Bookstore ☐ School Bookclub
   ☐ School Book Fair ☐ Other:_____

6. Have you recently borrowed any paperback books from
   your: (Check One or More) ☐ Friends ☐ Parents
   ☐ Public Library ☐ School Library

7. What other paperback titles have you read in the last six
   months? Please list titles:_____
   _____
   _____

8. Who are your three favorite authors? _____
   _____
   _____

9. Do you read magazines regularly? (Check One) ☐ Yes ☐ No
   Please list your favorite magazines:_____

For our records, we need this information from all our Reader's
Panel members.
Name:_____
Address:_____ Zip_____
Telephone: Area Code (   ) Number_____

10. Age (Check One): ☐ 10 to 11 ☐ 12 to 13 ☐ 14 to 15
    ☐ 16 to 17 ☐ 18 and over

11. Check One: ☐ Male ☐ Female

12. I am a: (Check One) ☐ Student ☐ Parent ☐ Librarian
    ☐ Teacher

13. I enjoy reading (Check One) ☐ Fiction ☐ Nonfiction books
    about (Check One or more): ☐ Friendships ☐ Romance
    ☐ Sports ☐ Humor ☐ Mystery/Adventure ☐ Science Fiction
    ☐ Teenage Problems ☐ Other:_____

Thank you for your help! Please mail this to the address listed
below.

NEW AMERICAN LIBRARY EDUCATION DEPARTMENT
1633 BROADWAY, NEW YORK, N.Y. 10019